The 2017 Scythe Prize

Short fiction, essays, and creative non-fiction

by college writers from around the world

Edited by Eric Forrest

Rusty Scythe Publishing
1719 N 131st Circle
Omaha, Nebraska 68154
www.scytheprize.wordpress.com

Ordering Information:
An initial print run will provide the publisher with a limited number of copies. Books can be purchased from the publisher or on Amazon.com

For details, contact the publisher at the address above.

Printed in the United States of America

Publisher's Cataloging-in-Publication data
Forrest, Eric.
The 2017 Scythe Prize: short fiction, essays, and creative nonfiction from college writers/ Eric Forrest

ISBN 978-0-9969852-3-9
1. Anthologies – Fiction – Essays. 2. Creative Nonfiction – college writers.

This book is dedicated to the editor's many Jewish mothers.

Table of Contents

Stories

Essays

Introduction

What the editor attempted here was to select some number of diverse, quality, and thought-provoking pieces submitted by college student authors in an attempt to share and celebrate their work.

That said, The Scythe Prize's goal is two-fold: to provide an opportunity for college writers and to release a book that is worth reading, discussing, and analyzing like any other form of high-literature is subject to. Upon analysis and measurement, we all hope these submissions prove worthy. What is more important is recognizing the young woman and man who allows us to share in her or his art.

In this second edition of The Scythe Prize, you'll find about two dozen of the best college-student-written pieces taken from hundreds submitted in the initial months of 2017 from roughly 130 colleges and universities around the globe. In the last two years, about 400 students from 35 countries on six continents have sent their best attempts to Omaha, Nebraska, and me. These two editions are my best attempts at sharing some of our youngest talented authors with you; people who will read our work here and elsewhere in the future.

Please read to enjoy and read to support these prospects looking to get a cup of coffee in the big leagues- maybe more. Let's hope appearing here in this humble book from an even humbler publisher aids them in building a platform and gaining confidence needed to become stars on the page.

Eric Forrest
Publisher and Editor of the 2017 Scythe Prize

Stories

Meagan Lucas
Southern New Hampshire University
Winner of the 2017 Scythe Prize for story

Kittens

Despite a grocery cart full of boxed mac and cheese, hot dogs, and hamburger helper, the calculator on Cheryl's phone indicated there was a miraculous ten dollars left in the budget. She leaned over the cooler, bright fluorescent light reflecting off the plastic wrapped meat. After endless ground beef casseroles, Tim deserved a steak. She ran her index finger over a line of white fat through the tight cellophane as her phone began to chirp and vibrate in her other hand.

"Hello," she said after the third ring. "Yes, this is she." The voice on the other end of the line told her what she'd been expecting for five years. "Thank you," she said, disconnecting and pressing the speed dial for Tim immediately.

"Hey Baby," he said.

"I need you to pick up the kids from school and take them to my parents." She scratched harder at the plastic, writing his name with her fingernail.

"Well, good afternoon to you, too."

She could see his brows coming together in her mind's eye. "I'm at the grocery store... and then I need you to meet me at the ER."

He blew out a sigh. Static crackled in her ear.

"You left her alone?" he accused.

***

Their daughter Hannah had been thirteen the first time the call came. Despite the heat of the July day, Cheryl's body felt encased in ice. She thought she'd freeze to death, hypothermia taking her on the ride to the hospital. Each subsequent time, she'd felt it less. Now, she was sweating.

That first call, a lifetime ago, they'd made a thousand excuses. Hannah was naive. She was just a kid. She was confused or pressured or didn't really know what she was doing. The second time, at fourteen,

1

Cheryl was suspicious they were wrong. At fifteen, they'd made the flying trip to the ER three times, and found her themselves a fourth. Tim had stumbled upon Hannah and a friend, prone and blue lipped in her bedroom. At sixteen, Cheryl and Tim spent half their life savings on rehab and still found themselves in the ER twice and at the county jail twice more. At seventeen, they spent the other half of their savings, plus some, on promises that she would change. But the only good that came from their overdrawn account was they believed for those few precious weeks she was safe.

***

The Emergency Room waiting area felt like home. Cheryl's bum knew the seat; she no longer heard the slide and screech of the door. Memories of teaching Jack long division under the hum of the florescent lights; of watching Annie text her crush; her legs dangling over the side of the plastic chair; of reading to Ben from the ratty book he found in the filthy children's corner filled her mind. All of her children together, shallowly distracted, their worry for their sister, for their lives as they knew them, hovering just under the surface.

"Have you heard anything?" Tim asked from behind. She hadn't seen him come in.

"Not yet."

He sat down beside her, resting his elbows on his knees. She studied the thinning patch on the back of his head, the crease across his neck, the way his shirt clung to his shoulder blades. Holding on to hope had turned her hair white, and rimmed her mouth in tiny lines; it had stolen the hair on Tim's head. Cheryl couldn't remember the last time she saw him naked. They hadn't always been like this. Saving Hannah was killing them.

"Were the kids okay at my parents?" She asked, wanting to break the silence.

"They knew why they were there."

"Well, of course..." Cheryl closed her eyes so he wouldn't see her roll them.

"But yes, Ben especially was excited about the kittens."

"Oh shit, I forgot about the kittens."

Cheryl rubbed her temples. Non-skid shoes squeaked towards them. She looked up and into the earnest eyes of a middle aged doctor, the corners of his mouth turned down. His hands were clasped in front of his abdomen.

"Mr. and Mrs. Davis?" His eyebrows went up.

She nodded.

"Can you please come with me?"

***

Money was always tight. They'd lived paycheck to paycheck with a hundred or so to spare. "Just in case" money they'd called it. In case she forgot to pay a bill, in case something small broke, in case of a field trip or group gift they couldn't wiggle out of.

Oxy and heroin were expensive. Not the drugs themselves, as Cheryl had recently discovered, they weren't a classy high. But cleaning up their mess was financially devastating. Cheryl could still remember the first time Hannah went to rehab, the feeling in the pit of her stomach when she checked the bank balance before she went grocery shopping. Her shock to discover she had to feed the family for a week on twenty-three dollars.

The kids were amazing. They didn't once ask for fancy shoes or the sparkly new toy advertised during Saturday morning cartoons. Yet, Cheryl lived in fear of birthday party invitations, school fundraisers, and car problems. She felt like a bitch for being so focused on money. It wasn't like her. She was a generous person, but it wasn't just dollars the drugs were stealing from their family. It was the way that Jack's foot tapped under the kitchen table when Hannah missed family dinner. How his lips were always chapped and his test grades plummeted. The way Ben liked to make a fort behind the curtain in the front window - the coldest place in the whole house, but with the best view of the driveway. Annie stopped eating. Cheryl would take treats to her at midnight when everyone else was sleeping, hoping to tempt her shrinking daughter and put some meat back on her bones. Her heart broke when she would find Annie curled up in her sister's empty bed.

They worried what Hannah had was catching. That one day they'd come home to one of the other children glassy eyed in front of the television. Or that their home would be mistaken for a drug den and would attract tweakers or the police. Fear was their constant companion.

***

"I'm so sorry." The doctor said, after they'd sat in the chairs and the broad expanse of his desk was between them. Cheryl looked down at her hands and traced her rough cuticles with the side of her thumb.

"I'm going to leave you alone to process this. If there is anything you need, please let me or my staff know." He left the room and took the air with him.

Tim stood and paced, ran his hands through his hair. Dark rings emerged from beneath his arms. He finally stopped, facing away from her, studying the doctor's diploma.

"What do we do now?" His voice was quiet and low.

"Well, I'm sure there is paperwork, and I have a car full of groceries, and we need to get the kids..."

"No, I meant..." Tim turned and shook his head. "Wait, what? You checked out at the grocery store? You got the call and then you waited in line?"

"I didn't have anything frozen, and we need to eat."

"She's our daughter."

"I pushed her out of my body..."

"Oh, so this is how this is going to go? Who loves her more? Who is hurting more?"

"I was going to say I remember exactly the moment she became mine. She was still inside my belly. It was the middle of the night. I don't know why I did, but I started singing. Ha! You know me, I don't sing. But I did then. You are my sunshine. And she kicked. It was the first time she had. It was the first time that it hit me that a person was in there. A person who was mine. I couldn't sleep that night with the weight of that responsibility pressing on me."

Cheryl didn't know when she'd started crying, but water was dripping from her face. She used her sleeve to wipe it.

4

"I remember too the moment that she slipped away. Last year. She'd been home from rehab for two months. I took her to get our nails done to celebrate sixty days of sobriety. I was bursting with pride. This was the time she was going to beat it. I was a good mother. Everything was going to be okay.

"Do you remember? We thought she was actually holding down a job?" Cheryl snorted. "We had conversations! She helped around the house! Two good months tricked me into believing. Then she got up from the manicure chair to wash her hands before they put the polish on. I was gushing to the nail lady about my brave daughter and all my dreams for her when Hannah's jacket on the back of her chair made a strange beep that I'd never heard before. I reached into the pocket and pulled out her phone. The screen was full of notifications from a messaging program I'd never heard of. I opened it. I scrolled through screen after screen of messages. We weren't stupid. We'd been monitoring her phone, watching the bill. When she told us she wasn't in contact with her old friends, we believed her. But we'd been duped. She wasn't sober, she was just better at hiding. All the money and hope we'd spent on rehab had just taught her how to lie better."

"Why didn't you tell me?" Tim's arms were crossed tightly across his chest.

"When she came back to her seat and saw me with her phone, she just shrugged, picked up her jacket and phone and left. We didn't see her for a week. I couldn't stand to tell you."

"Why?"

"Because we'd been so hopeful. Because it was my fault."

"It wasn't." He pulled her into his arms. It was the first time they'd touched in more than a week. Cheryl's skin sucked him up like a sponge.

"I know that now. I know that she made the decision. But for the longest time I blamed myself that I couldn't fix her."

"You can't fix her."

"I know." She laid her head on his shoulder. She inhaled the scent of the detergent she used to wash her family's clothes. He put his hands on her arms and pushed her away until he could look into her eyes.

"You're not surprised this happened."

"Are you?" She asked.

He studied her face.

She crossed her arms in front of her chest. "It was only a matter of time." She whispered.

***

Cheryl finished the paperwork while Tim picked up the kids from the farm. When she finally got home she could barely move her shoulders for the knots of tension in her neck. She left the groceries on the counter. Tim sat in the dark family room, the glow of the TV an eerie green on the wall. Ice cubes clinked in his whiskey glass. She was sure it wasn't his first, but it was promising that he was still using a glass.

Mounting the stairs, she felt guilty that she didn't want to check in on the kids. She felt guilty in her relief; shouldn't this be the worst day of her life? She didn't want to see the hope in their eyes or answer their unspoken questions. Tim had agreed breakfast was the best time to tell the children. Let everyone get some sleep. Maybe it wouldn't be as terrible a conversation to have in the morning. She craved a deep bath; ached for hot water stinging her skin to her chin and the random slurp of the overflow drain. Jack and Annie's doors were closed, but Ben's was always open, he was afraid of the dark. She crept by and heard only silence. She smiled as she pushed her bedroom door open. She wasn't a bad mom to wish for some alone time.

She kicked her shoes off into the bottom of the closet.

"Mama?" a small voice called from her bed. In the light from the hall she saw there was a tiny lump right below her pillow.

"Benny! Why aren't you in bed?"

"Where were you?"

"It's too late baby. We'll talk about it in the morning." She scooped him into her arms and carried him to his bed.

"What happened to the littlest kitten?"

She'd known this conversation was coming. She might be able to make him wait until tomorrow to hear about Hannah, but Ben wasn't going to let her off the hook about the damn kittens.

"Well, Benny," she took a deep breath. How was she supposed to explain the facts of life to a six year old when she barely understood them herself? "Sometimes, in a litter of kittens, there is one that isn't strong enough and the Mama kitty abandons it. You see, if that one is sick and can't make it, it's better for the others if it goes away."

"Where does it go?"

Cheryl was sure that her stomach was on the floor somewhere. It had fallen so fast and violently. "Don't worry about that, Papa took care of it."

"Is it always the littlest one that is the weakest?"

"Oh no, Sweetheart. You never know which one it's going to be when they are born. As they get older you can just tell because that one needs more help, more food, more attention, and still can't do what the others can. It will never be able to take care of itself."

"Why doesn't the Mommy just give the kitten more food?"

Cheryl was glad it was dark in the room. He couldn't see her broken heart or the tears streaming down her cheeks. "She does. She gives that baby everything she can. Even taking food away from the stronger kittens, but soon she realizes that if she keeps doing that, they will all die. To protect the whole litter she has to let one go. But you don't have to worry about it, okay kiddo? The rest are going to grow big and chubby and strong, and maybe we can go back to the farm and play with them tomorrow. Okay? Sweet dreams, little love."

Cheryl kissed Ben on the forehead and pulled his covers up to his chin. She walked to the door and blew him a kiss.

"Mama?"

"Yes, baby?" she answered, although she had nothing left.

"Is Mittens going to be mad at Papa? What if she changes her mind? Won't she miss her baby?"

"With her whole body. But Mittens knew, sweetheart, she knew what needed to be done, that's why she left that kitten alone." And before turning and crossing into her bedroom where, to the empty room she added, "She would save the rest, even if it killed her."

Simone Aliya

Vermont College of Fine Arts

The Avocado

On Thursday evening, the man brought home an avocado. He cut it open, salted it, and shared it with the woman. They sat at the round wooden table in their grayish–blue kitchen in the suburbs of Ohio. The woman couldn't remember the last time she'd witnessed such a perfect avocado. Most stone fruit she selected was overripe, underripe, bland, or damaged. One week earlier, the man had said that she'd do better were she to pay closer attention to detail. "I'm sick to death of bad avocados and peaches," he'd continued, "and of waiting so long for my fruit to ripen." That night, in bed, he'd repeated himself before turning off the light.

Fearing the words "sick to death," the woman had tried harder. She groped and inspected the avocados and peaches as she saw other women at the Safeway do, asked the teenaged produce clerk for assistance, and read the articles the man printed off the Internet. She learned that an avocado was ready to eat if it yielded to gentle pressure. Peaches matured well in brown paper bags and refrigeration slowed their ripening. Shriveled stems indicated a fruit picked too early, lacking fresh flavor and good texture.

But no matter how she studied, the woman improved little. "It isn't difficult, Leanne," the man had said on Sunday upon surveying a slimy, grayish–brown avocado she'd cut open for him.

"I guess I'm just plain rotten at it, Larry," she'd tried, hoping that her self-deprecation would gratify him as much as the perfect avocado might have done.

But he hadn't even smirked. "I'm simply too tired after work to stop at the store," he'd said. "Shouldn't a decent, hardworking man get to come home to a decent piece of fruit? And so the woman bided her time. "I have terrible cramps," she said each morning that week. "I can't go out." But while he worked at the Styrofoam manufacturing company, she went to the Safeway and bought only stone fruit. Until she had delectable avocados and peaches to offer the man when he returned home, she didn't want him to know she'd shopped at all. To hide the evidence of her repeated failure, she wrapped the remains of unsatisfactory offerings back in their grocery bags before tossing them in the garbage. Whenever she closed her eyes, she saw stems, skins, flesh and pits.

As she experimented, the pit of the woman's stomach itself became truly unsettled. "It's just indigestion from tasting the bad fruit," she told herself even though it wasn't the first stomachache she'd had following the man's reproach. At her core, she experienced burgeoning feelings at once of desperation, inadequacy and resentment. She sensed that, along with his condemnation, these emotions were sickening her more than the fruit itself. Did he intend to make her ill over something so trivial? "That's a truly rotten idea," she said to the molding peach she cut open, its flesh oozing like a pestilent sore. On her apron, she wiped the sticky brown juice from her hands.

"The avocado is perfect," she said on the Thursday evening the man brought home his gift. Perhaps remorse had led him to trouble himself to stop at the store. She had no appetite but ate the avocado anyway.

"It was two dollars," he said. "Two dollars for an avocado. Can you believe it?" She preferred discussing issues more global than the Safeway's fruit prices.

"Ecosystems are being destroyed by toxic chemicals used to produce roses," she'd reported to the man one bland evening, looking up from her news magazine. "People are dying," she added. At forty-two, the woman read to stay engaged with the world as she'd once been. In her twenties, following in her sister's footsteps, she attended nursing school and then worked full-time at a community health clinic in Florida. After at last admitting to herself that inspecting people so closely disconcerted her, she quit and started a new job behind the front desk at a Comfort Inn. She married the man shortly before her thirtieth birthday and switched to working part-time at the hotel upon his request. She found herself doing things like controlling the algae in his tropical fish tank and, to feel purposeful and valuable in a different context, volunteering at the weekend charity events hosted by her friend's non-profit organization.

When she and the man moved to Ohio for his old job at the insurance company five years after they married, the woman had worked for a city councilman's failing campaign. As the man's expectations of her at home became all–consuming, she slowly reduced her hours before quitting altogether. In her little spare time, exhausted from freshening linens and thumping rugs, she sat on the couch reading about the hardships of distant, oppressed communities. The disturbing stories of impoverishment not only helped her stay engaged but also offered her perspective, making it easier for the woman to feel satisfied with her small life that revolved more and more around the man and his host of endless domestic tribulations.

"Avocados are out-of-season," the woman finally brought herself to say on the evening he brought home his offering. "Sometimes fruit is more expensive when it's out-of-season. That might also be why many of them are spoiled inside." She paused. "What luck you had with this one, though."

"Well." He swallowed his last bite. He leaned back into his chair and studied the avocado pit. He looked at her and smiled. "You don't know anything about fruit." The woman stared at the small, withering cactus on the windowsill above the kitchen sink. Was watering it one of her little jobs? It occurred to her that she'd been forgetting to smell the fruit before purchasing it; she'd read that sweet-smelling fruit indicated perfect ripeness.

"But you know about everything else at the store, which I don't." He paused. "I don't know about anything other than what produce is good. Or bad."

Then why hadn't he also brought home a peach or two?

"But all of it seemed so expensive," he continued, as if reading her mind, "which is why I didn't buy anything other than the one avocado. I decided to let you keep spending your allowance on our groceries while I continue saving to buy us one of those nice, big houses in Chagrin Falls." He tilted his balding head and blinked at her. "The houses have balconies, Leanne," he said. "You'll get to fold laundry in the sun."

"Yes, Larry," she said. She hated folding his drab clothing. "It will be even nicer than our last house."

Before the man lost his job at the insurance company one year earlier, they'd mortgaged a home with hardwood floors in a suburb where women wore cashmere sweaters and hired Guatemalan landscapers. She and the man now rented a carpeted, split-level that smelled of the last tenant's kitty litter and was too close to Wendy's and the Interstate. She remembered standing beside him in front of his old fish tank the first evening in their downgraded living situation. Collecting unemployment benefits hadn't brought in enough money to avoid foreclosure or credit card debt. Along with the waterbed, he'd had to return the fancy aquarium he'd bought only days before the lay-off and place the "disappointed" fish back in their old home. "Remember that I married you because I'm attracted to your charm and ambition," she'd said. He'd grumbled about algae and then something about "the economy" and walked away.

But at her core, the woman knew that she'd also married the man for the sense of empowerment that was offered her by satisfying him. He'd always been demanding but had also made her feel valuable by praising her when she met his expectations, which had at one point been more often than not. All her life, she'd been average in everything from looks to sports and had come to consider pleasing others her talent, passion, and purpose. As she became unexpectedly isolated in her marriage, the woman found herself relying entirely on the man's appreciation of her. But, sitting across from him at the kitchen table that Thursday evening, she couldn't remember when he'd last commended her or touched her body gently as one touches a promising peach. Surely not since they'd received the doctor's news that she was infertile and wouldn't bear him the children she'd secretly never desired.

The news had arrived shortly after his lay-off and, in the months that followed, the woman had attributed the man's acute displeasure to his small paychecks from his new job at the Styrofoam manufacturing company as well as to his unspoken sadness about her infertility. She felt guilty and, craving his approval, feared appearing defective to him. Instead of rejecting his coldness and criticism, she resolved to reject the notion that his taste for her was rotting beyond her control.

Now, at the kitchen table, she reminded herself that feeding him the perfect stone fruit would bring the man such pleasure that things would return to the desirable way they'd once been.

"You didn't have to buy even this one avocado," the woman said. "You've been unwell," —— he clenched his jaw —— "and I was trying to do something nice. Can't a man do something nice for his wife?"

"Yes, Larry," she said. "It was very nice of you. Thank you." She wiped her mouth with the square of paper towel that was on the table. He said it was his, so she went to get him another from the kitchen and saw that the roll was empty. She searched for napkins, but they didn't even have the cloth ones used for company, since they never had company. The only people who called them were telemarketers and, in the past, her mother and father-in-law asking when they would have a grandchild. The woman brought him a dishtowel and sat in her chair. Tomorrow, she'd smell the fruit for long moments before daring to purchase it.

"I forgot to mention that we're out of paper towels." He dabbed at his mouth. "We seem to always be running out of things."

"I'll put them on the list for when I'm well enough to go out." She hiccupped, lowered her eyes, and traced a coffee ring stain with her index finger. She regretted eating the avocado. "I'm really very sick."

"And my bunions hurt so badly that I wouldn't trouble myself to go to the Safeway again even if everything there were free." He stood and walked to the kitchen sink with the knife he'd used. He reached to turn on the faucet, retracted his hand, and set the knife in the sink for her to wash. "Stone fruit isn't difficult, Leanne," he said, turning to face her.

The woman rose and tossed the skins into the trash on top of the fruit remains. Her stomach now felt as rotten as it had not only when the man reproached her, but also when she worked hard to conceal condemnable things from him —— emotions or receipts, spoiled peaches, her defects and even his own. She moaned softly.

"You haven't quit your medication, have you?" the man asked. She took antidepressants to treat what he called her "malaise," which worsened in the winter, Ohio's bleak sunlight as unfulfilling as weak tea. She missed Florida.

"I'm sick, Larry," she said. "People get sick."

"But you're sick so often," he said. "Why don't you go to the doctor again?" The woman hesitated. "I feel too wretched to leave the house," she said. But the truth was that she despised wearing one of those sad paper gowns and getting poked and prodded. She'd always feared a person somehow opening her up to discover, examine and reveal any kind of rottenness that was inside of her. "There's nothing physically wrong with you other than your endometriosis," the doctor had said the last time she'd visited, several months earlier. "It's winter, and you recently learned that you're infertile," he'd said. "I think you're also depressed and that your stomach pains are psychosomatic. Here's a prescription, my dear."

"See, this is why it would be pointless for you to have a job even if it was necessary," the man now said. "You'd be too sick to leave the house."

"I was never sick when I was working in Florida." She paused. "I loved working there. I loved working, period."

"And I love coming home to a nice, hot meal," he said.

"And I loved having my own paycheck to buy my own damn news magazines," the woman considered adding. She'd always deemed it sincere, masculine pride that drove the man to claim that he made a sizable income at his new job, that they lived where they did simply because he was saving to buy them one of the "nice, big houses" in Chagrin Falls. "I don't need you in the sky, Leanne," he'd once said, crumpling up her application for a position as a flight attendant. "I need you at home to improve the deteriorating quality of your housework," he'd added. Now the woman remembered finding the pay stubs that had fallen out of his briefcase, quickly tucking them back in their hiding place to protect him. She allowed the memory to dissipate her growing resentment toward the man, who she suspected was as insecure as she was.

"Other than the dryness of your roasted chickens," he continued, "you've become a very decent chef from reading those cookbooks my mother gave you. It's a shame we've been eating so many frozen dinners these days." He walked to his aquarium in the corner of the kitchen and stared at the dead fish floating on the water's surface. It occurred to the woman that she'd been forgetting to weigh the fruit; she'd read that heavier fruit indicated juicy ripeness.

"I'm feeling better." Her stomach clenched. "I'll fix dinner."

The man exited the kitchen. Soon she heard the local news reporter on the television: *The Whistler is on the loose again. Residents of an otherwise quiet neighborhood outside Akron reported disturbance by a whistling vagrant* – She turned on her personal radio. *Studies show that turmeric has anti-inflammatory effects and is a powerful antioxidant.* The woman changed the station and enjoyed a talk on various crimes against humanity while she fixed the man his favorite meatloaf using the last of their fresh ingredients. She changed the station again when the talk ended and a newsman reported a clown attacking mothers at a birthday party in Akron. "Oh for the love of God," she said. *Congressmen advocate for women and girls in developing nations,* the reporter on the new station announced. The woman listened, hoping that the man wouldn't intrude and turn off her radio as he sometimes did. The talks she enjoyed seemed to unsettle him.

That night, the woman stood naked in front of the bathroom mirror. A dim fluorescence cast a bluish-green pallor onto her white belly and breasts, untouched by the sun since she'd left Florida. As she applied gentle pressure to her abdomen, it felt overripe in her hands. She wasn't fat, but she'd gained weight as what she guessed was a side effect of the antidepressant. If she improved her figure, perhaps the man would want to go to bed with her and be pleased enough that she could forget about stone fruit. She'd have time and energy to get involved in the community and do the elliptical at the YMCA.

But then she recalled how draining it had once been to shed pounds and stay thin and how, for purpose and validation, she'd shifted her focus to helping others. Now – a childless housewife – she pursued the same objectives solely through establishing peace at home with the man. But, at her core, did she feel more or less passionately about her home and the man than she'd felt about raising money to support victims of monstrosities? Did she even have a core? She felt the urge to grab the man's razor that was on the sink and to cut herself open. Instead, she dug her nails into her plump belly and dropped her arms. She was too sick to focus on anything other than fruit-management. Tomorrow, at the Safeway, she'd smell and weigh the offerings.

The next morning, the man sat up in bed as soon as his alarm sounded. "I had a nightmare that the Democrats took over the country and forced everybody to pay higher taxes," he said. The woman had dreamt of forcing the man to swallow a peach pit, which she'd read contains poisonous cyanide.

She said nothing and lay in bed watching him dress in his beige suit. She moaned softly as her stomach clenched. Despite her inexplicable disinterest in motherhood, she wished that what she felt growing inside of her was a new life. Wouldn't a child to greet him at the day's end appease the man? She thought about how the perfect avocado had a pregnant woman's shape.

He sat on the edge of the bed to pull on his shiny black shoes, which she'd never failed to polish to his satisfaction. Even now, it pleased her to see what she thought was a shine in his eyes when he put them on. "Today's the day you'll see a doctor, Leanne."

Was he concerned, or was he simply "sick and tired" of her being sick? "I'm sorry, Larry, but I'm truly too unwell to go out." She rolled onto her side to face the window. A meek ray of light reached its long, thin arm through the gap between her hand-sewn, floral–printed curtains that the man had recently said belonged in a cheap motel room.

"Maybe it's a parasite." He grunted as he tied his laces. "You can get a parasite from all that bad fruit you eat." He seemed happy to say this to her.

The woman rolled onto her back. Had he somehow discovered the remains in the trash? And what if he was right about parasites? Perhaps it would be wise to admit her inadequacy. "I've been doing more research," she said instead. "I think I know where I'm going wrong."

"If you can do research while you're so ill, I'm positive you can drive to the doctor's." He rose from the bed. "And then to the supermarket as I bothered to do for the avocado." He stood in the bedroom doorway and smiled. "You'll feel better after you visit the doctor."

"How are you so sure?" she asked. She truly wished to know what could make a person so certain of things. Did he never question himself?

He frowned. "You test a man's patience, Leanne," he said and closed the bedroom door softly. No, she wouldn't forfeit her mission. She'd drink tea, eat Saltine crackers, feel a little better and drive to the store. Things would return to how they'd been before the man got sick to death of her bad avocados and peaches.

But how had things been before? Prior to her poor fruit selection, he'd fixated on her unsatisfactory wallpapering jobs and, before that, on the dryness of her roasted chickens. Maybe their relationship was rotten and they needed to discard it. She'd return to Florida, eat the oranges she loved, wear bikinis and reclaim her job. But her weekly allowance wasn't even enough to buy a bus ticket, was it? She'd have to get a secret part-time job and save money, which would keep her from completing her daily chores – the folding, tucking, scrubbing, kneading and slicing. She also recalled the man's random declaration months earlier that she wasn't a "spring chicken" and would fail to attract anybody as decent as he was no matter how she tried. She was too sick to think about any of it today. And she couldn't bear the man children, for God's sake. Shouldn't she at least be able to offer him the best stone fruit?

After she heard his car pull out of the driveway, the woman got out of bed, put on the kettle and shuffled to the living room, where she found *Home and Garden* on the coffee table in place of her news magazines. She and the man didn't even have a garden. Did he want her to plant avocado and peach trees? She envisioned the trees bending to a breeze in their small backyard that was carpeted with the moldy leaves she'd failed to rake before the first snowfall. "Don't be stupid," she said. "Those fruits don't grow in Ohio." Where were her magazines? Her stomach cramped, and she sat on the cheap white sofa that the man insisted on protecting with plastic.

She turned on the television and listened to the blonde newswoman: *In a quiet, family neighborhood outside Akron, another garden gnome has gone missing from resident Margaret Hill's* – The woman turned off the television. She looked out the window at a little boy riding his training-wheeled bike up and down the dead end street alongside the dirty, early-spring snow banks. The sky was porcelain white, and a conspiracy of ravens shrieked at the ground. A plastic bag twisted first one way and then the other in the branches of a tree. The kettle whistled.

In the pantry, the woman found her box of English Breakfast tea empty. "Oh for crying out loud," she said. She was almost positive yesterday's teabag hadn't been the last, and she would have recycled the box if it had been. And if the man had suddenly quit coffee that morning and started drinking tea, why hadn't *he* thrown away the empty box? She peered into it as if expecting a teabag to rematerialize. Was she delusional, or was the man tinkering with her sense of reality? On his desktop computer, she typed into the browser "how to know if you're unstable," then deleted it and replaced it with "how to know if your husband is unstable." She deleted that too. Wasn't he simply a disgruntled, balding businessman suffering from having no child, promotion, friends or hobby?

A cockroach scuttled across the carpet at the same time as her stomach cramped, and the woman researched "how to know if cockroaches are making you ill." She read that diseased roaches could give her Polio and next researched "Polio symptoms" and learned that she did not, in fact, have Polio. She tore herself from the computer chair. She'd eat a few Saltine crackers to gain the energy she needed to settle herself.

Even though she hadn't finished the remaining sleeve the day before, and the man disliked Saltines, the woman found no crackers in the pantry. Had he suddenly changed his taste, or had he tossed her Saltines that morning along with her magazines, her tea? She checked the garbage but found nothing. Perhaps it was the Garden Gnome Thief who'd changed his taste and was now targeting their home. Back at the computer, she again researched "how to know if you're delusional." 1. *Do you talk to plants?* "No; I only have the one cactus and don't even water it," she answered. 2. *Is Elvis Presley alive?* "Oh for Pete's sake." 3. *Do you have a conspiracy theory?* Before she could answer the eighth question, the doorbell rang.

At the door, two blonde young men wearing suits and carrying bibles said they were Jehovah's Witnesses with an important message for her. As they stood beside each other, shifting from foot to foot, she wondered if they'd ever persuaded anybody to convert and what would happen to them if they failed or ever challenged The Watchtower Society. The way they clutched what she thought were silly, ineffectual bibles comforted her. With her faith in the power of perfect stone fruit, the woman was surely less delusional than these young men who believed in an Armageddon. The damp, March air adhered to her bones, and she shivered in her nightgown. "This isn't a good time," she said and closed the door.

In the kitchen, she stepped on something slimy and sat at the table to remove a peach peel from the bottom of her bare foot. "Oh dear God no." She'd been so careful to hide the evidence. Without success, she tried to imagine the man finding her peels and, to protect her, disposing of them and saying nothing just as she'd silently returned his pay stubs to his briefcase.

Daylight was disintegrating even though it seemed the man had driven away only moments ago. She put on her coat over her blue nightgown, left the house, walked to the bus stop on the street corner, and stood in the freezing rain waiting.

This afternoon, in a Target parking lot in Akron, a man attacked a girl with a meat cleaver, a reporter said on the bus radio.

"Did you hear about the pro-life activists that marched outside Planned Parenthood today?" a lady on the bus said to the young man seated beside her. The woman covered her ears. She didn't want to consider the dangerous place the world was becoming for women everywhere.

The teenaged clerk who'd failed to help her earlier that week joined her in front of the avocados at the Safeway. He glanced at the nightgown that showed from under the hem of her coat and that she'd noticed too late. He pointed at a nearby stack of strangely translucent, yellowish fruit. "Those star fruit are really sweet and juicy," he said. "They're in season." He paused. "So much is out of season right now. These avocados, for example." He waved his hand at the neatly-stacked, little green devils. "You can get lucky, but it isn't worth the trouble."

The woman's stomach roared. Suddenly hungry, lacking strength for battle, she turned away from the avocados. She'd simply offer the man a delicious star fruit and tell him that the clerk had declared everything else to be out of season. She'd perfectly roast him a chicken.

"Please select me two star fruit to be eaten this evening," she said.

18

Waiting in the checkout line with the star fruit and the groceries she'd at last succumbed to purchasing, the woman read the tabloid headlines on the rack above the gum and candy: "Housewife Claims Baby Abducted By Male Alien!" and "Akron Meter Maid Attempts to Suffocate Husband!" What about men who disempowered and tyrannized people? The news seldom sensationalized the insane, unjust behavior neither of these men nor of the men whom they made desperate for security and relevancy. Meanwhile, despite social and political evolution to the contrary, too many modern American women spent their lives oppressed by power- hungry men – their own desperation spiraling until they went mad and arrived at the supermarket wearing their nightgowns. What was the difference between such women and the impoverished communities living under dictatorships? It crossed her mind that she perhaps should have gone to college. She might know nothing about stone fruit, but she was intelligent, wasn't she?

"Ma'am," the clerk said. "Ma'am," he said again. "How do you want to pay for your groceries?"

"Oh," the woman said. "Cash. I'll pay with cash." She opened her wallet and saw that it was empty. On how many rotten, two-dollar avocados had she squandered her cash? She'd have no money to buy groceries until Monday, when the man disbursed her weekly allowance. But what if he gave her nothing at all, assuming she still had this week's money from having supposedly stayed home? She had no choice other than to confess and to face the full extent of his condemnation for having lied, wasted his money, and still failed to offer him what he craved. But wouldn't he then fixate and maximize some other of her perceived deficiency? Dear God, maybe he'd have her re-wallpaper the bathroom again. "Nobody wants to sit on the toilet staring at shit-colored walls," he'd said about her sixth selection of paper.

"I don't know the way out," she said to the clerk.

The clerk frowned. Patches of dry, red skin surrounded his mouth. He pointed at the automatic doors as they slid open for a young couple holding hands, walking together into the wide–mouthed night. Automatic doors always opened as readily for the woman as they did for everybody else, which never failed to surprise her. "Will you still be paying with cash?" the clerk asked.

"I'm sorry, Sir," — the woman watched the doors open for a young, purple-haired woman, "but, as it turns out, I have no money." The contemporary American woman always had a choice, didn't she? She could select any life she wanted and choose again if it wasn't what she'd hoped it would be. Like a shade snapping up to let in the brightest light, the notion that she perhaps no longer desired her husband startled her. Why was she continuing to choose the discredited role of the repressed housewife whose husband offered her nothing other than insecurity and guilt? And for what did she have to feel guilty? It had been the man's parents and never he himself who'd expressed an acute desire for her to bear him children. It occurred to the woman that she didn't have to think about herself as underripe or overripe, pitted or coreless. She wasn't an object to be desired or discarded.

With four hundred and ninety seven dollars in her wallet from pawning her wedding ring, the woman sat on a sticky bench in a Greyhound Station that smelled of onions and old tobacco. She looked from the giant clock on the wall to the ticket kiosk; it was half past eight o'clock. Soon the bus would arrive, and she'd need to make her decision. She closed her eyes and pictured the man returning home from work and fumbling with the coat rack. He'd sit down on the sofa to watch *Jeopardy!* or *Wheel of Fortune*, checking his watch once, then twice. "It's enough to make a man crazy," she imagined him saying. "Is she trying to make me crazy?" Then she tried to imagine him making a start at understanding, suffering regrets. As he'd once done years earlier after he'd critiqued her figure at the dinner table, and she'd vomited and left the house for hours, perhaps he'd call her and attempt to reconcile himself.

And the housewife who had failed even in buying a star fruit for her husband considered all the women of Akron who were losing their minds over small, imperfect things. Then she opened her eyes and waited.

Lindsey Campbell
Southern New Hampshire University

Promises, Promises

He was always hanging out with my mom, and she was always trying to get me to hold his hand, so one day I just tried it. I didn't make a big deal about it, just took a breath, heard myself saying it, and then repeated what I heard.

"Hi, Dad," I said.

And ever since he gave my mom that funny look, and she looked at me and then back at him and I could tell that she was trying to tell him something without saying it, just like she's always telling me something without saying it. So I just knew it was over between us, even though it had never really started between us. But now it would never be there between us. Except for my mom, she was between us.

Steve was short and compact, sort of skinny but really heavy. He had a small nose and big ears so I started seeing him as a jack rabbit. When he was annoyed, he would twitch his nose back and forth, thump his hind leg on the floor, and sniff really fast. His quick movements alerted my senses, because I was *vigilant*.

Vigilant, like knowing my habitat, and seeing everything that moves, and smelling the fear in Steve's breath when he huffed and shuffled away from me. Predators are vigilant because they protect themselves from other predators. I saw it on PBS.

On the hot July nights of my tenth summer, they would wake me up, their noises penetrating my space. Sometimes there would be arguing, and then a late night kerfuffle, and then the night noises.

I would lay in my bed in the dark, the pink of my curtains faded into deep obscure purples, the ratty pastel carpet turned a bottomless dark lake of shadow, and hear their muffled laughter filter through the particle board walls. I would stare at my window frame immersed in moonlight, and beyond into my little square of sky, ashamedly eavesdropping on the breathless gasping, giggling and whispering, wondering why mother should love something so strange.

I remember trying to disappear into my pillow, the soap-and-sweat smell of my hair as I tossed and turned, clasping my blanket around my ears

21

and neck despite the heat, wanting the purple shadows to consume
me, praying for lightening to strike me deaf, a tingling between my legs
followed by extraordinary guilt, wondering how love could sound so
violent and grotesque, not believing that love was violent, or grotesque.
Wondering what exactly I was hearing. Not love.

I would wait for the lip smacking and groaning to stop. Then I would go
about my business, and make my nightly phone calls.

On that one night, the special night, I heard something different. They
didn't make weird noises, but were talking: *We are gonna move into a bigger
house.*

I perked up in my bed. All the sounds were very sharp: the crickets
outside the window, the chittering of flying critters by the roof, the far
away bark of dogs, the *shush* of cars on the highway miles distant, my
heart thudding in my head. I stretched my neck and strained to hear.

Steve, nasal and slithery: *I'm gonna get a good job, and buy some land.*

I crept from my bed, toes first, then dared a full foot, stopped for a
trembling minute in panic; when my mother's soft voice issued through
the wall once more, I made my move, stealing my way through the heat
across the room, like a night predator across a moonlit meadow. I knelt,
ashamed, with my knees on the carpet, slowly brought my hands to the
wall adjoining my mother's, and leaned my ear close.

My mother's voice was milk. *I can't believe this. It's like a miracle.*

After a moment of unintelligible discussion and soft laughter, I
abandoned that post and slunk slowly toward my open bedroom door on
hands and knees. I moved with the stealth of a crouching fox, hunting a
rabbit in the purple-black darkness.

He said: *Maybe we can get married.*

And my mother's voice dribbled: *Can you see a bump yet?*

The hallway floor was peeling stained wood, and the splinters raked my
knees. But the lone fox didn't flinch. Purple shadows embalmed me in
silence, and I tracked the course to my mother's bedroom door in furtive
solitude.

Her door was open just a crack. I postured in the shadow, where no light touched me. A dim lamp ray shimmered from within, and I could see Steve's hand grasping my mother's bottom, and his hips cradled between her spread legs. She looked at him much differently than she looked at me. Her eyes were soft and bright, the lines in her forehead relaxed and almost invisible, her dimple pouting softly from her flushed cheek. He excited her very much. Like a tinkling bell of glowing golden laughter, she gazed into him blindly.

The lone fox raised her hackles. The lamplight threw shades of red across the ceiling and floor. The man's hand moved to my mother's belly, and he patted her like a steak.

He said: *We're gonna get a real house. No more mobile homes.*

My mother's lips were like rose petals brushing sand paper when she kissed him. I grated my teeth.

She said: *We can get some milking goats, and a piano.*

I shifted my weight imperceptibly to my other leg. Her arms went around his neck, greened by old tattoos, stringy muscles sticking out. I imagined sinking my fangs into that flesh, the fibrous ligaments snapping between my jaws, my mother screaming in agony and joy as I saved her from the wretched rodent. I would shake him like a rag doll, his blood purple in the night, and howl at the derelict moon.

Someone said: *We're gonna be so happy.*

I wondered if there was room for me, too.

I knew there would be no milking goats, and no piano. Just like there were no ballet lessons, no silky tutu, no pink toe shoes.
Promises, promises.

They began to push their lips together and I turned my eyes away and swiveled my ears toward them. Something had changed, my fox-senses told me; something so minute as to be dismissible, yet dark and threatening. The triangle had been thrown off balance, the fulcrum moving off-center ever so slightly, the weight transferring away from me and toward the edge of a steep river canyon, her feet dangling precariously above a cliff over which I couldn't see, but I could feel that she was suspended over a cold, black abyss. I wanted to scream to my mother, *Look out! Grab my hand!* But she just kept laughing and laughing.

The rabbit nibbled my mother's neck, and she petted it, cooed like a dumbstruck invalid, her beautiful brown hair clasped between its ragged toes as it pawed stupidly at her chest. I turned away.

But that was my special night.

Through the woods I stalked, around the shadowy sofa, deftly between the trunks of the dining room table, under the dense canopy of the kitchen counter, reached my hand behind the refrigerator, and found the piece of paper with the numbers.

It was going to be my special night. Promises, promises.

As usual, I watched the clock and waited for the big hand to be on the six. 11:30. Now.

I leapt with grace and ease to the corner table and snatched the phone receiver. I rolled into a protective posture, my tail back, my neck parallel to the floor. No sound.

The paper was old and wrinkled and although I knew those numbers by heart, I clutched it like a weapon. If my mother found it, she would have made us move again. I dialed the numbers.
Listened to the ring. One ring. Two rings.

"Hello?" said Richard. "Hi," I whispered. "Hey, kiddo."

"I'm ready," I whispered.

"Did you pack your tooth brush?" asked Richard.

"Yes," I said.

"You know what to do?" he said. "Yes," I said.

Silence. His breathing. Then, "You sure you want to do this?" "Yes," I said.

I need to hear you say it," Richard said. "I want to," I whispered.

"You want to what?" "Go with you," I said.

"You gotta say the whole thing, kiddo. Just so I can be sure."

I took a deep breath. Silence from the hallway. No movement. "I want you to come get me." A sigh. "Alright, little one. We're going to do this. Tomorrow. You remember where?" "Yes," I said.

"If anything happens, you call me immediately." "Okay," I whispered.

"Is your hair still curly just like mine?" "Yes," I whispered.

"Your grandmother can't wait to see you, you know," he said. His voice was soft as a warm hug. I breathed into the phone. Just hearing his presence.

"And hey," he said. "Yeah?" I whispered.

"You can call me Dad. Since I am your father. When you're ready." "Okay," I said.

"Get some sleep," he said. "Goodnight. Dad."

Click. Vigilant.

Crouching, I lurked back into the hallway, my paws soft on the floor. I stalked back to my den, past my mother's bedroom door, the light now off and her bed bathed in purple-black shadow. I flicked my ears in dismissal, a lone pup cast from her pack, a runt, ready for fight, ready for lonely, ready for long winters ahead. Promises, promises.

The purple shadows welcomed me, and I swam the lake of carpet to my bed, where my pillow was soft, and my blanket was light, and my crickets sang lullabies, and my nightlight was the moon, and I would never make my late night calls after this night, and I would never pull my mother from the cliff edge, and I would never have milking goats or a piano, and knowing this I pulled my blanket tight around my temples like ear muffs and wrapped my tail around my feet.

Philippa Holloway
Edge Hill University (United Kingdom)

Light Up

Ada was smoking with her eyes open. Clouds of nicotine billowed around her head in the cold air like empty speech bubbles as she leaned against the back doorway of the shop and stared out into the easy drizzle, flicking ash sideways from the hip. There was no one there to see her drawing in the heat and holding it in her chest like an emotion before letting it leak slowly away to mist silently into the clean wet air.

The cigarette was an excuse, a chance to escape the shop for a while, to get away from invoicing and customers asking about the latest homeo-pathic trends or trailing their brightly clothed children through the aisle of dried fruit snacks, their voices floating through the aisles like dragonflies.

A flurry of sparrows bathed in a puddle across the road, flitting in and out between the scattered overflow from the bins. She thought about her own bath the night before, how she had seen the shape of the face in the patch of mould on the slope of her bathroom ceiling. Their conversation in the night, and Max. She thought she should feel sad, but instead inhaled relief between the smoke and the cool air of the street, picked absently at the flecks of white paint on her fingers with her free hand, and smiled.

The sky was clearing to blue and white even as she drew breath from between her fingers, glancing at her watch to see what time remained and stealing another half breath that brought the orange glow right up to the filter and her fingertips. She squatted down and dipped the stub in a puddle near the doorstep before tossing it into one of the oversized bins and heading back inside.

Max leaned across the office desk, pulled the document from the printer and glanced at it quickly before sliding it into an envelope and sealing it away, putting in his out-tray with the others. He ran his hand through his hair, caught the scent of the ink on his fingers, acidic and dry, as he massaged his tired eyes. It was only just after lunch but he felt the missed sleep from last night like a hood over his head, heavy and rough. His eyes sought the windows and the air the city promised and he considered leaving early again, making excuses and wandering through midweek streets filled with unfamiliar shoppers, maybe visiting Ada at the shop and telling her about the candles, how they made him feel. But he had to catch up with yesterday's missed work. The smell of wet paint haunted his senses and he went to find coffee, something temporary to numb the new feeling now settled in his stomach so that he could finish his day at work and get back to her.

She always smoked with her eyes open unless there were people around. If there was anyone there to cloud her vision then she would close herself behind her lids when she inhaled, an elongated blink to block out their faces. When she was alone her eyes stayed wide, blinking a mere reflex. She went straight to the tiny staff toilet and washed her hands, inspecting her fingertips and nails for signs of yellowing before hitching up her green embroidered tabard and drying her hands on her jeans, leaving two dark wet prints on the tops of her thighs. Putting the kettle on in the tiny office she leaned back against the narrow worktop and counted all the sounds she could hear through the shop, the hum of the refrigerated units near the front of the shop, a bus releasing air from its brakes on the street, the schoolchildren shouting to one another on their way home. Eventually the roar of steam recalled her attention and she poured the still bouncing water into her mug before adding milk and watching the water go blind. Finally she scattered in a teaspoon of fair-trade coffee, each dark brown rock turning black on contact before trailing off onto tiny caramel comets on the surface and sinking into normality. Moving slowly into the shop she carried it to the checkout counter and left it to settle while she wandered around tidying up the already neat shelves. Two regulars shopped together, women who sought out the same products weekly, knowing where to go and where to find the treats they'd share together later. She watched their closeness, the currents of understanding which flickered between them, and wondered what it would be like to share her life so closely with another woman, a mirrored self to space out the hours in step, but even as she wondered she held onto her own silent moments tighter. She had Max and he knew her well enough, letting her keep the rest of herself her own and sharing only the moments they chose together. Last night had changed things, made things clearer. A smile danced across her lips for a second and settled in her eyes, and she forgot about the face and thought only of Max. It was enough.

She had finished work early the day before and so walked the back way home, avoiding the school children and their calls for sugar, their wide pink mouths making her feel too tall, too wide for their space, as if she were in another country and didn't know the language. She turned back into town and the high street just to head to her flat. Its doorway, invisible to the shoppers who passed in droves, led to steep stairs and her own private front door. The steps were dusted with crumbs from the fresh bread she often bought from the baker's on the corner and couldn't wait to eat, its golden crust beckoning to be bitten. She would hold out until she was off the street and out of sight of the human traffic, then bite into the crust with her teeth bared, exposing the soft white cotton wool flesh beneath and scattering crumbs like Gretel on a walk in the woods.

That afternoon she had no bread. She thought about going out to get some later, when the street was clearing, an offering for Max for when he finished work and came over. But she wanted only the silence of her hallway and the ache of her thighs as she reached the top step and fumbled for her key in her bag. Later, after a bath and an hour or two breathing her own space and possessions in the almost quiet, later they would decide together on food, maybe wine.

Max had been standing at the cooker when she entered. He called out "hey babe," as he heard the key in the lock, but didn't turn to look, giving her time to frown and drop her keys into the blue ceramic bowl on the chair by the door.

"What are you doing here so early? Everything okay?" she said as she hung up her coat and ran her hand up the nape of her neck and into her hair. Her hand caught in the grey blonde curls and she winced and gave up. She pulled her sleeves back to just below the elbow and walked into the kitchen. Max kept his attention on the stove top, stirring something in a pan. Ada knew it wasn't food, could smell the hot wax warming the air around their heads like forgiveness.

"I told them I was getting a migraine. I needed to get out."

"Are you?"

"No. Well, no. Not anymore. I'm making candles."

"So I see." Ada smiled, her gaze taking in the curls of chipped wax and desiccated tea lights scattered like ashes across the worktops as she moved in to embrace him from behind.

"Hey, watch your hand Ade, you'll get burned," he said, stepping back a little from the hob and pressing into her. She turned her head and rested it between his shoulder blades, feeling the width of his shoulders filling her tiny kitchen. He stroked her fingers with one hand, stirring the hot wax with the other.

"I can't stop," he said, "it would either burn or start to set."

"S'okay, I'm going to take a bath anyway, wash the day off me." She kissed him on the spine and walked back into the hall to slide the bolt across the front door before heading for the bathroom.

"Why?" She paused by the doorway, unsettled by the sight of him at the stove, the ancient smell of molten wax. "Why are you making candles?"

"I don't know," he replied without turning, "I just felt like doing something different, making something, for us. I thought it would be fun." His hands moved carefully, absorbing each necessary flexion with grace, enjoying the sensations. Ada walked away silently, his vibrating enthusiasm threatening to draw her in and divert her from her predicted evening.

Steam had melted the bathroom into fog, softening the mirror and window and draping around her head and shoulders like a shawl. She chose an easy lemon fragrance to pour into the water, something to drown out the smell from the kitchen which was already filling the room with monastic air. The water was too hot as usual, and Ada lowered herself into it in stages, her skin turning red below the bubbles and itching with the heat where it met the waterline. She eventually leaned back into it, gasping, and waited for the particles of day to lift off her into the thick swirling air.

Closing her eyes against the artificial light she felt the hours stretch out ahead of her, long and narrow and filled with Max's broad shoulders. An uneasy feeling crept up her spine and she wanted a cigarette, wanted to block out her rising irritation at his early presence with that fragile weight between her fingers. She didn't want any candles. She didn't want him to move in without them noticing. She wanted the moments waiting by the window for him to come round the corner, the lift in her solar plexus which told her they would spend the evening doing nothing together, and that would be enough. She wanted the wide hours between work and Max.

Ada raised her hands out of the scalding water, guilty that she wasn't delighted at the extra time they had together, rubbed her eyes and face and wiped away beads of tingling sweat. She opened her eyes and looked up at the patch of mould that was staring down from the slope of ceiling opposite the bath. She had barely registered its slow growth over the months from just a shadow that had haunted her peripheral vision, but it had taken shape over the last few days, shaded blacks and greys that defined its features and stared at her through wraiths of vapour.

Even through the haze she could see that it had changed again, focussed its attention on details and depth. There was a perspective to the features now, an accent she wasn't sure of in the swell of the lip, the bruise of the shadows around the eyes. It was almost perfect, a recognisable face angled into the slope above her feet, looking down on her through the swirls of soft citrus steam.

Max lifted a plastic tub half full of molten wax out of the pan of boiling water and carefully poured its murky contents into an empty yoghurt pot. Across the pot lay a wooden cocktail stick with a piece of string tied to it that hung down to form the wick. He was careful to pour the wax slowly, keeping the string as near to the middle as possible so the candle would burn true when it was lit.

He had only ever made candles once before, years ago in the school holidays. Back then he'd been minding his little sister while his parents were out for the evening and at her persistent request had kept her entertained by following instructions from a magazine on how to make candles out of reclaimed wax and household rubbish. While helping him pour she had spilt some wax on her leg and the carpet, and although he had tried to deal with both as best he could his parents were furious to find both a ruined carpet and a blistered daughter on their return from the theatre. Clara still had the dark pink stain of scar tissue on her leg, although it had faded and was smaller than before. She often joked it was less of a concern for their parents than the ruined carpets, and they would laugh because it was probably true and they didn't mind.

Once the yoghurt pot was almost full Max moved it right to the back of the counter and set the plastic tub of leftover wax beside it, savouring the rich ancient scent so unfamiliar to him and yet comforting, relaxing. He wanted to make Ada a cup of coffee while she was still bathing, and so left the pan on the cooling hob and focussed instead on cups and granules and hot water in the usual order. Max's cups of coffee always tasted the same.

It wasn't until he was carrying both drinks, carefully, out of the kitchen that he noticed the absence of music from the bathroom. The flat was silent. He could hear only the noise from the street filtering through their boundaries. Usually Ada listened to the radio while she bathed, loud when she was getting ready to go out, or in the background while she read the trash fiction she kept hidden in the cupboard under the sink.

"Can I come in?" he called from the hall, even though the door was ajar.

"Yeah, sure," Ada replied, her voice loosened with steam and ringing out against the porcelain acoustics. Max's stomach relaxed and he was aware of the tension with which the silence had corseted him.

"I bear the gift of coffee," he said, pushing the door open gently with his foot, pausing to see if it would hit the side of the bath and bounce back to knock the cups from his hands.

"Thanks hon. Can you see that?"

Max set Ada's mug down on the side of the bath, turning the cup so the handle faced her. "Here you go," he said, and sat down on the toilet lid, cradling his own mug in both hands. "See what?" Ada was quiet again, frowning off at some point near the ceiling. "See what?" he repeated.

"Nothing," Ada turned to him and smiled. "Thanks for the coffee, you really are a lovely." Max smiled back and tried not to look at her nakedness through the dissipating bubbles.

Max slept. Ada left the safe walls of his body and slipped from the bed. She paused for a second to listen to his breathing, deep and clear, easy to sleep next to. She felt a shiver of guilt over her early irritation, thankful now for his solidness, his wide reality, filling her bed.

She glanced again at the bedside clock, illuminated numbers telling her how tired she would be in the morning, and then padded barefoot out of the bedroom and into the kitchen without putting on any lights. The streetlamps outside the lounge window lit her curtains to black, forcing a dense glow through the flat so that everything had the same colour and texture. Walking to the window she pulled back one curtain to look down at the empty street below. It made her feel like a child again. She closed the curtain to block out the invading emptiness and went back into the kitchen to make coffee, mixing the milk and granules into a dark pool while the kettle soothed her with its mammal purr. When it was close to boiling she lifted it gently off its stand and diluted the dark to light in sudden silence. She picked up her cigarettes from the counter and walked away from the lounge and the window's silhouetted threat.

Stepping into the bathroom Ada hooked the door closed with her heel before pulling the light cord with her little finger and shielding her eyes with her cigarettes, hoping the clatter of the old extractor fan didn't wake Max up. Gradually her pupils retreated behind her grey irises and she could see the hard white corners of the sink and bath, light refracting in spears. She sat on the floor and leaned her back against the door, holding her coffee in both hands, against her knees.

Eventually she looked up to the soft bloom of mould in the corner of the room. From this angle, and without the veils of steam, it looked clearer, chiselled. A strong brow and jaw, the promise of a cheekbone. She focussed on the peripherals, avoiding the eyes and then glancing around her looking for her cigarettes, finding them on the floor beside her where she had placed them only moments earlier.

She looked back up as she drew one from the pack, made eye contact as she as she brought the lighter flame to its tip, and then shut her eyes to take the first breath. Pause. Hold. Part lips. Relax. When she opened her eyes again the face was staring at her through the grey ghosts of her exhalation. She blinked and so did the face.

Ada looked down quickly, felt the burn of her coffee cup in the palms of her hands. She could hear a faint noise at the back of her mind and then realised it was her own heartbeat. She took a mouthful of coffee and fought hard not to look up, but she could feel the eyes watching her and she felt anger prickling the soles of her bare feet, working its way up to pinch at her sides. Eventually it reached her mouth and she looked up. "How long have you been up there, watching me?" Her voice was louder than she had expected, resonating back from the curl of the sink and the cool tiles. "For how many days? How many baths?"

The face looked down on her patiently and Ada tried to detect an angle of response in the shading at the mouth. She looked away, closed her eyes and sought intimacy with her cigarette and then let out a long curling breath that relaxed her and fed into her tiredness and the weight behind her eyes. She turned her gaze up towards the face again and calmly scrutinised it. The face looked back, passive and open, letting her examine it in her own time.

"You look familiar." She said, "Where? Where have I seen you before?"

The face smiled, a shift of shadows at the corner of a lip and the amusement was there, printed into the artex. Ada's cigarette was nearly finished. She took a mouthful of the cooling coffee and then claimed the last dying breath from her hand, holding it longer for its encore before letting go. She stood up and ran the stub under the tap to drown out its heat before dropping it into the pedal bin by the sink and washing her hands. She thought she should probably brush her teeth too, but wanted to savour the taste of her sins a while longer.

"Okay," She said to the ceiling, "I've got it. I know who you are. And now I think we should talk."

Max moved slowly away from a dream. For a moment the soft angles of the dark bedroom brushed shoulders against the disappearing images, but the voice was still there. He lay on his back letting his mind regroup, and then massaged his eyes for a moment with his fingertips, watching greens and blacks explode into geometry under his eyelids. He knew Ada wasn't beside him, that it was her voice he could hear through the wall, at once muffled but louder because of the hour and the absence of traffic at that time of night. Something must be wrong, and he knew he should get up and find out what was happening, who she was on the phone to in the middle of the night. Maybe someone was sick, or had died.

His body lay heavily upon him as the voice arced through familiar cadence. Quiet, then angry. A laugh. Silence. Conversational and yet clearly emotional. Pushing himself up on one elbow he ran his free hand through his hair then moved into an upright position, stretching his limbs out slowly into the deep air like an insect unfolding for the first time.

The flat was never really dark, but as he reached the hall, usually the darkest part for lack of a window, he could see a stain of light pooling under the bathroom door, soaking the carpet in colour and drawing him closer, towards the drone of the extractor fan and Ada's sweeping syllables.

As he passed the hall chair he saw her phone, lying mute by her keys.

Suddenly the bathroom door opened, catching Ada on the hip with its handle as she paced the cold floor tiles and causing her to curse, surprised and in pain from the blow. Max materialised from the darkness of the hall, eyes screwed tight against the brightness, reaching out for her with his arms. She swerved away from his embrace and stood between the face and the door.

"Max, what are you doing?"

Max slowly opened one eye and rubbed the other. "I heard voices. Are you okay?"

"I'm fine." Too fast. She bit her bottom lip and waited, watched his face smooth out as his eyes adjusted. She sat on the edge of the bath drawing his newborn gaze down, away from the sloping ceiling.

"Who were you talking to?" She half expected him to glance around, to search for her companion, but his eyes didn't leave her face. "Ade?"

"No one. I was talking to myself."

His eyes moved then, pinprick pupils searching the room in flickers, glancing off the shine of the taps and buffeting the towels on their rail over the radiator, alighting once more on her face. "It sounded as though you were having a conversation."

Ada looked right back, feeling the eyes watching the back of her head, un-accusing, observing the lie. "You must have been dreaming, I was just muttering to myself because I couldn't sleep and needed the loo again. Too much coffee I guess." Ada never put the bathroom light on for night time visits, she always left the door wide open so the streetlights' reassuring glow could pick out the room in pillowed shapes and let her eyes stay half rested and ready to resume their sleep on her return to the bedroom.

The back of Ada's head was starting to itch. She knew the face was watching her and her lie blazed on her cheeks. She wanted to turn around and lower her gaze, but instead she raised her hand and touched the slight dip above her sternum where a pendant would rest.

"Are you ill, babe?" Max reached for her again, kneeling on the floor in front of her, and in that gesture she felt ready to cry.

She leaned forward into his arms and closed her eyes. "I'm fine," she mumbled into his neck, "I'm just sorry." Max wasn't listening. She felt his neck stiffen as he gasped, pulling away from her, almost pulling her off the edge of the bath.

"Oh my god, Ade, there's a face on the ceiling, look."

Ada just nodded through her tiredness.

"Ade, look," he squinted, tilting his head to get a better angle. "It looks like…"

"It is," she interrupted, still staring at the floor. "It is."

Max sank down, sitting back on his feet and staring at the face. Eventually, without looking at her, he asked "is that what you've been talking to?"

"Who, not what."

"Sorry, is that who you've been talking to?"

"Yes."

Her eyes felt like they were filled with sand, so heavy she could barely keep them open. She got up and collected her cigarettes from the floor by the door, then sat on the toilet lid and smoked one in silence, keeping her eyes shut the whole time. Max didn't move. She could barely hear him breathing, could only feel his size filling her small bathroom with the aroma of sleep and fading body heat.

"Ada," he said eventually, "if it is, shouldn't we do something?"

Ada looked at him then, as though for the first time, looked right into the nakedness of his face and realised that he hadn't really seen it.

"Do what, exactly?" Her voice was measured, barely inquisitive.

"I don't know, tell the papers or something. People will want to see it, won't they?" He stood up and started toward the door. "I'll get the camera so we can at least take some pictures."

"No." Her hand reached out to stop him, pushing him gently in the stomach.

He looked at her face and saw the rawness, the eyes dark circled and older than he remembered, her mouth softened with sadness. Her cheeks held a flush he had never seen before, not even in their closest moments together.

"Go back to bed Max," she said evenly. "We'll sort it in the morning."

His own tiredness stirred in him, gritting his eyes and pulling down on his hands like weary children. "Okay, but you should come too, babe, you've got work tomorrow." He stroked a strand of hair from her brow and took her hand to lead her back to the bedroom and the shapes their bodies had left in the bed.

"I'll be there in a minute," she squeezed his hand and let go. "Go on, I'll be there." He nodded and glanced once more at the ceiling as he left, bare feet speaking barely a whisper on the hall carpet, the darkness of the bedroom folding him into its arms and rocking him back to sleep.

The alarm went off on the bedside table and Max rolled slowly to meet its birdcall with his outstretched hand. He didn't need telling twice. Real light filtered through the dark green curtains and he felt like he was waking up in a forest, the tremor of traffic on the street outside like the wind through pine trees. Ada wasn't there.

She had come back to bed after he had already fallen asleep, half woken him by wrapping her arms round his waist and pushing her damp face into the hollow between his shoulder blades. Her sadness had soaked into his dreams, moving like a flock of starlings and settling somewhere near his throat just before dawn. She hadn't woken him again.

He got out of bed and saw the evidence of her preparation for work. Her pyjamas were strewn casually on the floor, tabard taken from the chair by the window and comfy flats missing from where they had peeked their toes out from under the chest of drawers all night.

Heading for the kitchen he saw the empty coffee cup by the sink, the pale veined imprint of her mouth in lip balm on the edge, betraying which hand she had held her cup in, and which the first cigarette of the day. He imagined her fingers curled through the handle, palm burning to the balm of hot coffee. There was a post-it note stuck to the kettle with a scrawl of light blue ink across it saying *I'll cook tonight, love you.* Max flicked the kettle on and tipped a spoonful of coffee into the used mug before giving in to his nagging bladder and going down the hall to the bathroom.

It wasn't until he was washing his hands that he remembered the face on the slope of the ceiling over the bath and glanced up. It was gone. The patch of mould which had blossomed slowly over the last few months now glistened with wet white paint. He could smell it then, that just moved in, almost intoxicating smell of hope that fresh paint breaths into a room. Max stared for a while at the clean, innocent space, and finally bent his head to the sink to wash the sleep from his face. He shaved slowly, sharpening his jaw with each draw of the blade, then went back into the bedroom to dress for work.

When he returned to the kitchen he poured the hot water into Ada's mug and drank the coffee black in three mouthfuls. He set the cup down in the sink and collected all the candles he'd made the night before and took them into the bathroom, breaking open the plastic pots and placing the candles in the bath. He lit them with Ada's spare lighter, the one she kept in the blue ceramic bowl on the chair by the door.

Each flame crackled with new life for a second before finding its own height and shade of light and becoming still. Max ran a little water into the bath, enough to surround the candles without raising them to float. He knew they would be safe to leave, that if the wax spilled over the edge because the wicks weren't true it would solidify in the water like lava, that when they burnt down they would drown quietly and leave only tiny coloured islands that smelled faintly of loss.

He went back into the kitchen and picked up the post-it note, folded it three times, placed it in his back pocket and left for work, breathing in the sound of the awakening city and holding Ada's sadness in his forgotten dream.

At the shop Ada measured out small bags of dried fruit, labelled them with their weights and cost and thought of the bread she would buy for Max on the way home from work that evening.

Krystal Lau

University of California, Los Angeles

I Wonder If He Ever Got Away

Every night I go to the gym, I see this same guy. He radiates intensity–bulky in-your-face muscles, screwed-up face, hair-like needles sticking into his scalp. He's a bit older, middle-aged, but you wouldn't guess that. By the way he moves he acts like a teenager, shooting up like a beanstalk. Like every time he takes a step, he's surprised by how much body there is.

I go the same time every night: nine o'clock on the dot. It's well after dinner, enough time to digest, and the moment you're back you can shower and hit the bed. A good arrangement, as I see it, but Frank sees differently.

It starts on an average Tuesday. "Do you mind if I work in between your sets?" he asks. We'd passed more than a dozen times before. We had that sort of familiarity that comes from recognition, but nothing more. He'd nod at me, acknowledge my presence, then go back to his routine. Gym dynamics were strange that way.

But then, he breaks it. The unspoken rule. I let him switch machines, but that isn't the end of our brief interlude. Turns out he has quite a mouth on him. And he uses it.

"Come here often?"

I know that he knows the answer to that question. I answer him anyway. "Just as much as you do."

He has a grunting sort of laugh, caught between pain and relief. As I find out, it matches his personality, his pained way of being.

"Gotta be dedicated to come this late, when half of America's on the couch watching the telly." He thumps his chest for good measure, radiating pride. "Sets us apart. We're not quitters; no we aren't."

A not-so-sly way to compliment himself. I smile politely. I think he likes that response; it gives him room to go on.

"Me, I have to be here every night. If I'm not– don't feel right. Not at all. Need the gym like I need air." He smirks like this is a good thing.

"Everyone needs a break sometimes," I shrug.

He hoots a full-belly laugh. From across the weight room, an elderly woman shoots us a glare. Frank ignores her; I start to inch away. "No, I don't catch a break until I reach my goal. I have a goal, you see. Set in stone."

"Good for you."

He leans in with a conspiratorial air. "You look at me now, you see this flabby guy, right? Overweight, balding, probably mid-life crisis you're thinking. Don't lie to me; I swat lies like flies."

I can't help it; I laugh at that. He isn't offended though. If anything, this encourages him. "Most guys– they end up like this forever. From here on out, it's bozo to the grave. But me? I'm not like the rest of them. I'm going to change. I'm going to have that perfect Brad Pitt look at fifty, and all the girls will come swooning. Not that I'd care; I'll do it for me, see?"

He seemed so genuine there, his eyes misty with a faraway look, I couldn't help but wish him well. "That's great," I say, and I mean it. Sure, his dream is a bit vanilla, but at least he has one. Me, I try on hobbies like clothes.

He ruffles his feathers, running a hand through his sweaty hair as he flexes. "Well, better get back to it. Best of luck."

From then on, it's more than just a nod or two. Frank goes out of his way to greet me, and I make sure to wave or smile or offer some form of acknowledgement. I see what he needs: recognition. Appreciation for his efforts. He wants applause. He wants an audience. Fortunately, or unfortunately, the gym is pretty empty at night. All he has is me.

This goes on for a few months. I get busy with college apps and life, and don't work out as often as I should. Still, sometimes I imagine him there, counting his sets in pig-like grunts, his breath whistling in and out like a wavering breeze.

Life evens out in spring. I return to the old gym like a pilgrim coming home and, sure enough, I see him there again, pounding out the treadmill with the vigor of a chef kneading dough. Each of his steps the beat of a war drum.

"What's up, Frank?" I call out.

He jabs at the decelerator and slows, a huge Cheshire grin spreading across his face. "How you doing?" he yells over the whirling fan.

With an enormous huff, he towels himself down. I watch the poor white cloth turn to pulp. His head is a raincloud, and his sweat a puddle pooling around the machine.

I give him a basic rundown of the going ons. He nods, attentive, then launches into his own soliloquy. How easily we fall into step, I think. It's as if nothing's changed.

By the looks of him, nothing has changed. He still has that unfortunate flab around his belly, that gut that won't go away. He tugs at it every once in a while, a nervous habit of his. Every time his belly gets in the way, his eyes pop in surprise, as if he can't believe it's still there. Frank has a good six feet on him, but his bulk drowns out his figure. The muscle blends with fat, so that you can't tell where one ends and the other begins. I just call him a big guy. It does the job.

He slaps his gut just then, his thoughts heading in the same direction. "Here's the deal. This little guy here just won't seem to go away. It's not like I deserve it. I don't even do anything; I work out every day, don't eat nothing."

"You don't eat?" I ask. It isn't that I'm worried, but... Frank seems like the kind of guy to go to drastic measures.

Frank opens his mouth, then closes it. He sucks in his cheeks; his eyes grow beady like a bird's. "Well," he begins, in that characteristic drawl of his. I wait, knowing a story is coming.

Sure enough: "You know I don't eat dinner, right?"

"Why not?" My eyes flit to the sluggish old clock in the corner. Its hour hand ticks feebly towards the number ten.

"Dinner's my only meal alone in the day. And once I start... I can't stop." He chuckles, but there's no humor in his eyes. "It's like, the little guy's an alien, you know? And once it's gets control of my mind, I'm possessed. I can't think; I literally can't think. And then I'm just consuming– the food's going in a mile a minute. Everything you can think of, everything in the vicinity. I just don't get it; I literally can't stop."

A desperate urgency creeps into his voice, a change so gradual I

40

don't notice it until it's fully formed, choking his lungs like a fist around his throat. "Afterwards, after all the food is gone; I wake up. I open my eyes, and I see the devastation around me. And I just can't figure it out: *what happened?* I just don't understand. I don't understand."

"It's okay, Frank." Awkwardly, I extend a hand and pat his sweaty arm.

"I think I'm cursed, I really do." He lets out a long shaky breath. "But here's the thing; that alien picked the wrong guy. I'm no victim."

Here comes the puffed-up chest again. Relief trickles through me like cool rain. This is the Frank I know. "So I decided: no dinner. Just skip the meal entirely, and skip the brain-control. If I don't eat, alien's got no power on me."

"Are you hungry then?"

Frank shrugs one shoulder, the picture of calm. "Good days and bad days. Good days and bad days. After gym, I usually eat a snack. Just a snack. Studies show it's healthy, you know. Gotta replace that protein in your body."

I nod. "That's true."

His chin quavers a bit: the calm before the storm. I tense, ready to run if need be. My sympathy only goes so far. But he only smiles. "That alien's got no hold on me," he says again. I think we both need the reassurance.

Summer comes around and the gym empties like water down a drain. In a college town like this, half the population disappears during break, leaving the locals with rare peace and quiet. At eleven in the evening, the gym is practically a ghost town.

Tonight, it feels like one too. The eerie drip drip of a broken pipe, the soft laughter of a late-night anchorman, talking to himself in the corner TV. The squeak of rusty machines, the groan of tired treadmills anchoring themselves back into resting position. It's like the world has been turning, on and on, and now it's finally coming to a halt, a standstill, waiting to see where we'll take it. We all hold our breath this night.

A light drizzle starts shortly after ten. By the time I'm closing out my routine, it's pouring outside– ground-shaking, howling summer rain, enough to make you want to heave out your ark and prepare for a flood. The trees are bending this way and that like dancing shadows, and the lamplight pools and flickers against the cement, sending schisms across the puddles. With dread, I towel off and head towards my car. Luckily, I nabbed a close parking spot tonight.

Frank catches up to me just as I'm on my way out. I notice him by the concierge desk, his garish bright red shirt like a stop sign. I slow down.

"Hey, Frank."

"Reckon you could give me a lift?" he asks, his lips curling hopefully at the corners.

I tilt my head, trying to pass off my reluctance as thoughtfulness. The gym's empty as a morgue, and the weather outside means Frank would have to swim rather than walk home.

"Why not," I say. The picture of nonchalance. Frank thanks me with his usual enthusiasm, then sprints back to the locker room to gather his belongings.

The TV's still running in the corner, a bouncy infomercial recommending weight loss pills and other snake oils. I wait by the tattered leather sofas, reading the inspirational posters and trying not to inhale the over-whelming aroma of dried sweat. Gym membership spiked in January, the poster discloses. Unfortunately for Frank, July's hit an all-time low. His audience has dwindled down to one.

"Thanks for waiting," Frank huffs as he storms into the lobby. He catches sight of what I'm reading, then pointedly stands in front of it. That's like Frank; he needs to command all attention, or he's not breathing loud enough. "Ready?"

Frank barely has anything on him: a towel, a beat-up wallet he could fit in his pocket, a key switch.

"That's all you have?"

"I run usually," he explains. "Home and back. It's not far from here."

I whistle, impressed. By the end of my workout, I'm ready to collapse in my heated car, close my eyes and listen to the radio. Meanwhile, Frank is racing home each night, beating through the weariness and the dark, trying to outrun his little alien.

"I didn't think it would rain," he offers. Weather's a good topic, safe. As we cross through the gym door, we need it. It's strange territory, where we are. I've never seen him outside the confines of those sterile white-washed walls. He looks almost outlandish out here, a complete stranger against the waving trees and starless sky.

"The weather report didn't mention anything about rain," I agree. We run to the car, and I hurriedly unlock the doors, oddly nervous. I glance down to see if there's anything sharp in the passenger seat. I feel in my pocket for my phone: it's alive and humming, ready if need be.

Just for good measure, I check my messages as Frank settles into his seat, leaning the chair back to accommodate his thick frame. Just as I'm about to pocket my phone, the screen flashes with an errand reminder.

"Oh, Frank. I forgot: I need to pick up milk and eggs. Mind if we stop by the grocery store first?"

"Be my guest."

The store is only a block from the gym. Maybe it's part of their business plan; tired gym goers make for easy prey. It's late though, and neither of us are easy prey.

I head directly for the back, where they store the dairy. Frank loiters in the front, so I leave him behind. I figure I'll meet him when I check out.

Sure enough, I do. He pays the same time I do, so I get a good look at what he's buying. I bite my tongue to hide my surprise: big juicy burger, its bun crisp and golden, its meat glistening, laden with sauce. Beside it a cup of fries, burned on the edges, soft white on the insides. There's more. Extra-large milkshake, pink and innocent as a bowtie, frothy whipped cream spilling over the top.

My eyes rove down the checkout lane. Multiply that by three, and that's what he's getting. I try to meet his gaze, to understand what he's doing, but he doesn't see me.

"Do you want your receipt?" The cashier pulls me back. I shake my head– both to the cashier and to myself. It's not my business. Frank is a grown man; he does what he wants. I grab my milk and eggs, then catch Frank's eye.

To my relief, he smiles at me, balancing his wide assortment of food in between his hands. As we head out the store, the rain lessens. I get into the car, Frank right behind me.

The moment the doors slams shut, it's like a switch turns inside him. He tears open the deli bag and begins to consume. Consume is the right word; the food disappears like magic, like dandelion fluff in the wind, like condensation in the sun. I don't turn on my car, I'm that engrossed. I know it's rude to stare, but honestly I can't do anything else. It's no matter; he ignores me completely. The burgers and fries and shakes go down his throat like air; he doesn't even pause to draw breath. His chest rises and falls like the ebbing tide, so that this feels natural somehow, inevitable, as part of his life as the waning moon and the shifting waves.

The food's gone within minutes. Seconds, maybe; time feels immaterial. I don't speak. Neither does he.

Outside, the clouds part to reveal a crescent moon, thin as paper. Frank lets out a long sigh, and everything is normal again. "Sorry," he croaks, stifling a burp. "I saw the deli and couldn't resist."

"No need to apologize," I hurriedly say. "You must be hungry. I could never work out without food in my system."

He doesn't answer. We watch the windshield wipers, diligently swiping away rogue rain drops. The street lamps blur before my eyes like a sad movie.

"It's an alien, it really is," Frank mutters, so soft the words are almost lost in the rain. "I'm telling you, the alien's at it again." He pats his stomach fitfully, then stretches, his fists clenched like a child's. For a moment, I want to tuck him into bed and whisper goodnight. For a moment, I wonder if he ever grew up.

"Sometimes, I can hear it speaking to me," Frank admits. He stares out the window, pensive and forlorn. "I'm not crazy, I know it. But I can hear its little voice. It lives inside me, see, and it has this power I can't get back. It has this power over me, and it knows it. It uses it."

"Frank…"

"You think I'm crazy, don't you?" He peeks at me out of the corner of his eye, and I can tell he's not angry, only afraid.

"No," I say. "Just struggling– like the rest of us."

"Struggling?" he repeats, offended.

I sit up straighter. "Through life."

"Ah." He likes this answer, I can tell. Makes him feel a part of things, connected. Makes him feel set apart, superior. "The truth is everyone else struggles. But I overcome. You'll see: one day, I'll reach my goal. Almost there, you know."

"Good for you, Frank," I say, but I'm tired. It's close to midnight, and the rain is making me sleepy. I stifle a yawn as I key the ignition.

"I'm going to reach my goal. Just you wait. And when I do, I'll be a new person. Not a soul will recognize me. I'll shed my old self like a snake skin. And anyone who was around to remember– I'll leave them behind too. I won't let them recognize me, bring me back to this old way. No, I'll be done with that. I won't leave a trail– no breadcrumbs. It'll be a new me, completely. That way, the alien won't be able to follow; it won't find me."

I have no idea what to say to this. I figure shedding that snake skin includes me. Mercifully, Frank is quiet for the remainder of the ride. He strokes his belly, but makes no sound. He's in a thinking mood, only speaking to offer the barest of directions. When I pull up to the curb, taking in his squat, beige one-story, he barely realizes we've arrived.

"Oh," he exclaims after a moment, clambering to get his things. "Thanks for the ride." Still, he glances back behind him, as if we've arrived at the wrong house.

"Is this it?" I ask uncertainly. Frank pulls on his sweat bands, as if preparing for another long trek. "I can drop you off somewhere else if you prefer." It's still pouring outside.

Frank waves this off like a pesky fly. "Thanks for the ride. Appreciate it. Really do." As he gets out the car, I notice him glance over his shoulder again. He crouches to tighten his shoelaces.

I lean forward, my hands braced on the steering wheel. "Frank, are you going home?"

Pulling himself up to his full height, he prepares to argue, but then deflates, a sad soaked balloon in the rain. "Nah," he confesses. "I reckon

45

I'll run back to the gym, do another workout, run back, then call it a night."

"Frank, it's late," I protest. "You shouldn't overwork yourself."

"I'm going to beat this alien. You'll see. I'm not going to let it win."

"You can start tomorrow," I argue. "It's alright to eat unhealthy once in a while."

Frank shakes his head ardently. Raindrops bead in his hair like jewels, and he holds himself like a king. "That's what they all say. Tomorrow, tomorrow. They never start. That's why they never win. The thing about me is— I'm going to win." And there it is- that cockiness, that toothy smile, that mad glint in his eye that shines through the night.

I drive away still thinking about him, imagining his wet sneakers and his wet socks and his wet toes pounding down the pavement. His drenched T-shirt sticking to his flab, see-through against the streetlights. His dead-set eyes, hidden beneath craggy brows, a furrow in his forehead like a marked grave.

Life happens after that. Things get busy again. I pack for college. I prepare to move out. Gym is neglected as I move on. Eventually, I forget to say goodbye. I leave for LA and enroll in the university gym. It isn't until the following summer that I get the chance to come back, to pick up my old gym membership.

As I walk through the beaten red doors, the paint chipping on the edges, I take in the familiar scent of dried sweat and half-hearted air freshener. The corner TV is still stumbling on; the local anchorman's petering on and laughing at his own jokes; nothing's changed. The sofa's ripped upholstery. The outdated machines, creaky as a grandpa's joints. In the distance, the plodding drip drip of the leaky drain.

I go through my routine, same as usual. College has changed many things about me, but not my workout. As I run, I glance over my shoulder, keeping an eye out for a balding, heavy-set man. As I stretch, I peek in the mirror, watching to see if anyone passes. The faces are foreign, unfamiliar. The voices are soft, delicate. I don't hear that belly-busting laugh, that sound that never seems to blend in.

And then, just as I'm about to give up, I turn the corner and spot a man striding down the hall. He bears a lurid red shirt, much like the

46

one Frank in all his color-blindness used to wear, and his hair sticks up pin-straight against his scalp; even looking at it gives me the tingles. He easily clears six-feet, and his step is gangly, awkward, like a hormonal boy just getting used to life with long legs. But here's what makes me slow, what stops me from calling out: the guy is fit.

There's not a tinge of fat on him; he is raw sinew and muscle and bone. His back muscles ripple through the thin material of his shirt. His calves bulge with every step. As he swings his arms, I see the definition in his shoulders. I wonder, *did Frank beat his little alien?*

"Frank!" I call out, hastening forward. The man turns, ever so slightly – or did I imagine that? – and then straightens. He heads down the corridor without another moment's hesitation.

I hesitate, doubting myself. That didn't seem like Frank. The Frank I knew would show off his gains like Olympic gold medals and boast like Zeus himself. I wonder if I'm getting nostalgic, reading signs that aren't there. But there's no harm in double-checking.

I hurry after him, but when I round the corner, there's no one there. I spend the next few minutes searching the old gym up and down, but the man is gone. Disappeared. It's like I imagined him.

With a sigh, I head out the front door. The glass is still oily with fingerprints; I wonder if anyone could spot my own mixed in with the crowd. A sign that I was here, that I existed, if but for a short while. I leave my fingerprints, and the gym, behind. I get in the car. I start the engine.

In my mind, I see that man again, his back muscles rippling, his frame tall and lean. Maybe that was him. Maybe Frank did it. Maybe he caught his alien, and nabbed him. Or maybe he ran as fast as he could, and lost that little voice.

I never see him again. Not even a glimpse. Wherever Frank went, he was right; he doesn't leave any trails.

Still, when I'm back home, I sometimes remember him. One picture sticks in my mind. Not the cocky grin, or the heavy, look-at-me sigh as he drops his weight back into the rack. Not the guilty eyes, or the way his mouth opens wide when he devours his food. No, the one image I remember is Frank facing down the rain, preparing for the run back to the gym, and then the run back from the gym. I imagine him pounding down the pavement, the rain getting in his eyes, the cold soaking through his clothes, the weariness sinking into his bones. I imagine him shaking all of that off and going on, one foot in front of the other, determined to run from that little voice, that little alien, who in the end– was only ever himself. I wonder if he ever got away.

Rachel Wyman
Pratt Institute

Guédé

Months before I met Sugar, I bought a roll of easel paper, pinned a six-foot piece to my closet door and made a huge drawing of a gap-toothed man in a top hat and sunglasses smoking a blunt. He wasn't supposed to be a man, but a spirit in the Vodou pantheon called Guédé. I was learning about Guédé, Vodou, and all matters of spirit in a Haitian dance class that I chanced upon soon after moving to Brooklyn. I didn't notice for a long time, but my mind was changing.

I surprised myself, drawing Guédé. When I stepped back and decided the larger-than-life sketch was finished, I hardly recognized my involvement in its creation. I examined Guédé's staring face and wondered why. Now I see I had begun a very slow transformation. I think of that drawing as an invocation that caught the attention of some force I didn't know I needed.

I've always liked to put my finger on turning points. Identify the Why. Find a dangling thread and follow it back to its source, admiring how it connects everything along the way. I love being able to say *that was the moment. That's what brought me here. What made me this way.* It makes a story, and stories neutralize every good, bad and sad thing. They let you realize it's all there to be what you need.

The usual transitions and rites of passage have never featured largely in my personal narrative. Losing my virginity, moving away from home, getting a degree. Such signifiers of change don't interest me. When I think of pivotal moments, odd memories stick out. Years before I drew Guédé, for instance, I remember telling my parents that I wanted to quit riding horses. Looking back, I'm sure that act forecasted the end of my childhood.

I was eight years old when I started, with skinny legs and arms. I took lessons with a lady who lived in a trailer surrounded by wheat fields thirty miles out of town. She was big-hearted, had stray dogs, cats and guinea hens roaming on her land, and often brought up The Lord. I didn't know anything about The Lord, but miles away from town, sounds, and other people, I started to feel something I didn't know. A feeling like being nothing and everything. So comfortable in the air and land around me I would forget thoughts, identity and body. Evaporate in the sun and slip back into being the no body I vaguely knew I had been.

I remember many summer days in scorched dirt paddocks. Sweet animal smell, star thistle growing rampant. Creaking saddle leather, the sound boots and hooves make kicking up clods of dry dirt. Then, my favorite-riding bareback after a lesson. Feeling the sweat and heat of another being, so close that the body boundaries softened, sometimes disappeared completely. I couldn't be sure which of us was an extension of the other, baptized in a fine layer of dust.

The changes must have started before I actually quit, around when I turned fourteen. My interest in boys had probably grown enough to sicken me with the desperate want for a womanly body. Surely I was already getting pubic hair, breasts. But as far as I remember, it was the act of telling my parents I was done with riding that brought on puberty to sex me, possess me. The walls of my body, once so insubstantial, hardened and held me. Some unfulfilled instinct left me ill-at-ease and hungry, constantly dissatisfied.

Part of me believes that it all could have been prevented. My declaration was an incantation, a conjure that worked on me until I unwittingly summoned a new force with my drawing, a long way from wheat and horses. The root took hold in Brooklyn, where Guédé planted the seed. When I finally met him, Sugar germinated it, grew it until it filled me up.

***

I liked D the moment I saw her. She must have been six months pregnant when I walked into her class for the first time, but still dancing hard, *going in* as I would hear Brooklyn people say. I panted and puffed in the sticky June heat, thinking incredulously that I needed to start a training regimen if I wanted to keep up once D's baby was born. Aside from her perfectly round belly, she was long and lanky with high cheekbones, large dark eyes and biscuity brown skin. She kept her head shaved and habitually wore purple sweatpants with one leg rolled up to expose a slender shin. As she explained in future classes, the dances she taught were mostly connected to Vodou, and she was serious about dispelling misconceptions and ignorance.

"People be like, 'Vooodooooo!'" She'd say wiggling her fingers by her face and widening her eyes. "But Vodou isn't about sticking shit in dolls. It's a beautiful system. It's about getting deeper into your soul, deeper into the natural world. Serious stuff."

I admired D's dancing, her long elegant limbs. But I marveled at how

50

effortlessly she filled space and time with information – for the body, brain and whatever was in-between. I was a few months into my transplanted life, and New York was constantly reminding me of my ignorance. So I was surprised at how comfortably her teachings sat with me, even while being completely foreign. I began to understand the major Vodou spirits, and through D, they showed me new ways of moving. Their dances embodied principles and personalities.

I immediately fell in love with a dance called Yanvalou, for the serpent spirit Damballa and his wife Ayida, the rainbow. D explained that together Damballa and Ayida encircle the world without beginning or end, and Yanvalou's continuous spinal undulations symbolize timelessness and infinite presence. She demonstrated this with supernatural fluidity, sine waves traveling through her spine, shoulders and neck. Where one undulation rippled through her back and disappeared, another was already gathering underfoot, traveling up through her legs to resurface.

I couldn't imagine a body doing anything more beautiful. Learning to move this way was crucial. I undulated in my room, in the shower, in front of the mirror in the living room while my roommate was at work. I stood on trains and buses, trying to feel every subtle weight shift in my pelvis and spine as we slowed, sped up, rocked. Each time I practiced, my body found the undulation faster. After a while the movement became reflexive and thinking about it seemed disruptive. I surrendered thoughts to sensation.

In the last week before D went on maternity leave, Guédé appeared to end class in a brief, clamorous finale. The drummers started up with a rhythm so driving and staccatoed it was nearly frantic, and D took the last five minutes to lead us in a procession around the room. Her steps were light and fast, her pelvis loose. The dance had a sly personality, at least the way D did it. At one point she stopped to respond to a break in the drum rhythm. Rooting her left foot, she swept her right leg up and out to plant herself in the slightest of squats. Then, the punch line, she slowly lifted her pelvis in a suggestive grind and abruptly let it drop. It was sexual without being sexy, with D's execution so frank and humorous that it never became coy. She introduced the dance as Banda and the spirit behind Banda as Papa Guédé.

"My personal favorite. He's death, rebirth and regeneration. He sees the really big picture, so he can't take our emotional hang-ups seriously. Especially when it comes to sex. He's just pure creating energy, without the social expectations. He tears apart all the romance and sentimental stuff we put on it."

I watched D absent-mindedly rub her pregnant belly. "For Guédé it's like, 'Y'all got here somehow so don't even pretend.' Sex is creating power, and that's everything. When we do this little –" she marked the pelvic drop "– we're not just flaunting our stuff. We're asking for fertility. Maybe you want to make new life with your body. Or maybe you want to make art with your soul. Either way, we ask Guédé for those blessings."

She gave a small smirk, put her hands on her hips and said dryly, "Can't nobody run home tonight and put me on blast for hoochie-coochie dancing. Guédé is deep."

***

Growing up in a rural area, I didn't see hordes of people every day; I saw stretches of uninhabited land. The small slice of humanity I was familiar with seemed smaller, driving through miles of open fields on the way to my riding lesson each Saturday morning. I looked at myself and the people around me as random, unimportant characters passing in and out of a permanent landscape. The land had lasting value, but whoever and whatever we were was inconsequential.

In the city, people are everywhere and everything. The city tells people that humans and their doings carry the world's meaning. And because there are so many people and endless possibilities for different interactions, encounters feel significant. Destiny seems to guide every path.

***

Sugar and I could have intersected early in my new New York life. My first year in the city, I would only venture into Manhattan to visit a particular dance studio I liked, and Sugar owned a small store across the street. By day it was a somewhat inscrutable boutique proffering an array of vintage clothing and rare vinyl. In the evenings, when he wasn't toiling away on his own projects, he hosted happenings and workshops for artist friends.

Of course I knew nothing of those gatherings on the evenings I emerged sweaty and exultant from class to sway back toward the subway, open and receptive to whatever twilight spirits would have me. On how many occasions had I unknowingly heard his voice from across the street, mingled with other voices as an event broke up? How often had his deep, sweet laugh rolled over me and receded like a wave as I walked obliviously in the opposite direction? And how many times had our paths run parallel, had we not quite merged on the road?

Afterwards, I wondered why we couldn't have met sooner. Why Fate didn't guide me across the street one single time. Why I had to wait so long. I told myself it had to have happened that way.

***

My second winter in New York, I was underemployed, confused and stricken by seasonal melancholy and loneliness. I was doing the thing of desperately trying to form a life, while having almost no sense of what I wanted to be or do. All winter I drifted, duly seizing opportunities for work or sex, yet generally moving through the months without a snag of true joy or anguish to grab onto. By February, I needed grounding, a different kind of physical expression. Something that lingered. I found an art supply store and bought easel paper, then I went home and drew Guédé. Lying in bed that night, I examined him staring back at me from the closet door until my eyelids got heavy and I turned off the light.

***

As a kid, I was both deeply unsettled and fascinated by ghost stories and anything supernatural. I wanted constant reassurance that the spooky thoughts I came up with were trapped in my mind and couldn't enter the physical world. I was afraid just thinking of something made it real.

I couldn't help but think those thoughts, though. My imagination spun images and stories against my will, pulled from such unknown depths of mind that I believed I'd invented something out of thin air. Or that something had come to me from outside myself. Images, scenes. A revelation, a flash of insight, a spirit. Tucked into my bed in the dark, I understood logically that thinking of a ghost did not mean it was in the room with me. But my body didn't understand logic and its fear told me I couldn't be certain.

Almost every night I ran down the hall to my parents' room, trying to escape the solitude of my mind with its shape shifting thoughts and dreams. Seeking the solid comfort of real bodies, warm and breathing.

***

I thought I would die of relief when D started teaching again in the middle of March. Her first class back was salvation and rebirth. We did a series of agricultural dances to encourage the advent of spring – a Kombit Suite, D called it. In her earthy voice she sang *bonswa Kouzin, bonswa Kouzine oh*, greeting Zaka, patron spirit of farmers, vendors and all hardworking, salt-of-the-earth people. I was ecstatic, sweat disguising my tears of joy. Lost memories of square dancing in high school gym class resurfaced in sentimental light. I thought of all the boys at my school that wore Carhartts and camo, kept hunting rifles in their pick-ups and spoke with an unplaceable accent that might only be classified as "rural."

The days became longer. It rained a lot and got warmer; the smell of damp earth and new foliage refreshed some part of me that had become brittle. I felt better to be taking class with D again, but I still didn't know what I was doing with myself and all of the time invested in dancing. Believing that serious dancers are in serious companies, I went to various auditions under a cloud of obligation and dread. I found most of them unpleasant and a few depressing. So many bodies crammed together, identified only by numbers pinned on spandex leotards. I always felt heaviness in the air.

The concept of energy was still new to me as a recent transplant, so I didn't understand what I was sensing. Back home, I had never felt the emanations of so many people. Their desires, fears, failures, ambitions, intentions, visions, anxieties, nightmares, passions, wounds, mistakes, neuroses, schemes, delusions, grudges and hope-against-hopes, projected outward and mingling in different combinations, blessing the air of New York one day and making it heavy with grief the next. I was learning to discern other people's energy in daily life, but it was overwhelming at auditions. I couldn't separate my own self, my own feelings. Nervously stretching in the studio, my body's story one among all the others, I would sink into the collective illusion: my value as a dancer – and therefore as an entity, since dance was the be-all and end-all for every one of us – was about to be determined in the span of a few movement phrases.

***

I imagine the memories and information we accumulate as little streams that flow into an ocean of knowledge. If our minds were designed differently, maybe we'd see their boundaries and sources clearly. We'd know exactly when some piece of information entered us and where it came from. As it is, everything runs together. I'm forgetful. It seems so long ago, and so many memories have come to crowd this one that I think it must be warped. Clear, chilly day. The end of April, maybe. White shirt, buttoned all the way up, a felt hat tipped on his head. Dark. Wide cheekbones. Ethnically ambiguous eyes, like mine. A subtle exchange of gazes, a subconscious interaction.

***

He liked to tell me he was a genuine love child, a product of his parents' first passion. They were eighteen, still growing up even as they raised him. There was a lot of love between them, he told me. Many evenings he found them dancing to records in the living room. George Benson, Marvin Gaye. They were romantic.

"They separated for a while," he said. When I asked why, he was silent for a long time.

"They didn't know how to handle practical problems," he offered finally. "But they got back together eventually. They loved each other too much."

"They're still together now?"

"My mother is dead, but yes, even so. I was on the phone with my father yesterday. He said, 'I dreamed about your mom again last night. She was right there.' He dreams about her all the time. I don't dream as much, but I think about her."

"You were close with her?"

"Very. She was the one who always called me Sugar. Even when I was bad."

Aside from that, he asked many questions and spoke little about his life. This endeared him to me, since I, too preferred receiving other people's stories. I had learned that others would handle the talking if I asked a few questions and shut up. His immunity to this tactic forced me to tell him things. The things became stories as I spoke, and I listened to my own narrative with some wonder.

He turned every query back on me, opened me up while maintaining his mystery. I always went away feeling that he had stared straight in as I shamelessly revealed myself. He saw me and it felt good.

***

"What keeps you from doing what you want?" He asked.

"Self-doubt. Fear."

"That's honest." He smiled. I smiled back and shrugged.

"What do you want to do?" He asked. I was going to say I didn't know yet, but other words came.

"I want to understand things. But also find some peace with not understanding."

"Do you think your dancing fits in there somewhere?"

"It's everything."

"Tell me."

"I don't know how to explain."

"You do." I sat for a long time, sensing that there was an explanation, but feeling bereft of words. I didn't foresee the explanation that suddenly came forth.

"I read so many ghost stories as a kid, but they terrified me. I hated to think anything like that could be real. Things I couldn't see in the physical world...the idea was too spooky. I always loved physical things, dancing... things that felt solid." I stopped, trying to find the thread.

"And?" He prompted after a while.

"Now the more I dance, the less solid it feels." He waited for more, realized I was done.

"Now I don't follow."

"I don't know how to say it. It started feeling beyond my body."

"What does that mean?"

"I don't know."

"You have to stop saying that."

I sighed. He waited. "I told you I've been learning about Vodou?"

56

"Mhmm…"

"That stuff is all about invisible things. Everything that I would usually say isn't real, period. But the dances are so beautiful…the different spirits, the symbolism. The spirits supposedly come right to the floor, into people. Dancing! I love that idea."

"Have you ever been possessed?"

"No. I want to be. I want to know for sure that life isn't just what I can see. There's so much out of sight that I don't see, but that doesn't mean it isn't there. I don't understand anything."

He looked into my face with an indecipherable expression. I squirmed under his stare. After a long silence he said, "Do you know what you are?"

"A hillbilly in the city." I offered. He ignored my joke.

"*Authentic.*"

"What does that mean?"

"You're open. Maybe too open. You don't hide."

"Not from you." I gave him a shy smile, but he didn't respond. His expression remained unreadable and where before he felt so close and warm, he was suddenly remote. Then his face softened slightly.

"You need boundaries in this city," he said.

***

Vodou speaks of spirit possession as horsemanship. In ceremony, a person becomes *chwal* – the horse for an arriving spirit to mount and ride. The human body is necessary for spiritual contact, allowing "divine horsemen" to join the physical world and mingle with the living. But to enter the body, the horseman must displace its steed's consciousness. While everyone else enjoys the visitor's company, the horse wakes up with no precious memories. Just a tired body and other people's tales of what happened.

***

"When's your birthday?" He asked.

"December twelfth."

"Sagittarius," he said approvingly. "Warm fire."

"When's your birthday?"

"I'm a Leo."

"You won't tell?"

"It was last Tuesday. Don't suck your teeth at me, I don't celebrate birthdays."

"You could have said something. I wouldn't have made a big deal out of it. How old are you?" I realized I had no idea. I looked closely at his face. More than twenty, less than eighty.

"How old are you?" He asked.

"Twenty-five. And..." I counted on my fingers, "eight months." He pulled his driver's license from his wallet and showed it to me. I did a quick calculation. He had just turned forty-eight.

"I can't believe it."

"That scares you?" He asked.

"No. You look good." I added sadly, "I won't look that good in twenty three years."

"That makes me sound old."

"A number is just a number."

"That's true. You still like me?" The question surprised me, especially its hint of vulnerability.

"Why wouldn't I?" I wondered. He nodded. We sat in silence for a while.

"I never had birthday parties when I was little. I'm not in the habit of celebrating."

"Not even with family?"

"I don't remember when I was really young. My parents split by the time I was eight or nine and I went with my mom, so we kept it minimal.

Sometimes she would make a cake. Or my aunt would. Women always pay better attention to stuff like that." He smiled, looking lost. Then his face brightened.

"I forgot. I had this girlfriend in high school. I hadn't said anything to her about my birthday coming up, but I guess she knew. My seventeenth, must have been. We'd planned to go out, just go to a movie or something. But when we were almost to the train she said she forgot something and we needed to go back to her house.

I was like, 'What! All the way back?' Really annoyed. Turned out she planned this surprise party, gotten all our friends in on it. We walked in and everybody was there, she made a cake and everything. Man, they really got me...I had no idea. It was the only surprise party I ever had." He shook his head.

"She must have cared for you a lot," I said.

"Yeah. First girlfriend."

I tried to imagine the girl who planned his only surprise party, who lovingly baked his cake and delighted in his look of astonishment when the lights came on and everyone jumped out. I felt a pang of jealousy. When Sugar was seventeen and running around New York, I was still six years away from even existing. I couldn't decide if the thought made me feel better or worse.

***

Sugar always saw me home after we'd been out, but he never tried to come inside. He'd deliver me to my doorstep and plant a chaste kiss my mouth, the way my father used to kiss me before picking up his briefcase and heading out the door. I had a feeling he would never ask to come in. The choice would have to be unambiguously mine.

"My roommate is away." I told him under the streetlight. The air outside was finally cooling, drying my sweat. A jagged white band of salt had formed across the front of the leotard I'd worn to class and sported on our date. He noticed and lightly touched my ribs.

"Okay."

"Do you have to leave right away?" He checked his watch.

"No. I don't have to leave." He looked at me and waited, making no moves. I was uncomfortable asking for what I wanted, unsure what to expect from him.

"Will you come in," I finally asked, "and spend some more time with me?"

"Yeah. Let's see your nest."

I led him in. As I showed him the living room and kitchen full of my roommate's furniture, decorations and cooking equipment, I noticed that there was nothing of mine in the common space. My bedroom contained my few possessions, and they rarely spilled out of that boundary.

"Nice." He said as I opened the door to my room. He put his hands on his heart and crossed the threshold with a look of reverence. He gazed around and I watched, trying to see myself as he saw me. The plants on the windowsill, the dream catcher I'd brought from home hanging by the bed. The mattress dressed in old pink sheets, pillows bunched up to make a nest and a few books stacked nearby. My bureau with its piles and scatterings of earrings and necklaces, half-used bottles of scented oil and lotions, wheat pennies, and plastic hair ornaments.

All of it sitting in dust.

He looked at the small shrine I had recently constructed in a corner on the floor, my attempt at honoring the spirits I was beginning to know and love, along with my own creators and ancestors. I had amassed and carefully arranged pictures of my parents and grandparents, candles, seashells, heart-shaped jewelry and trinkets, crosses, beads and anything else that struck me as a nice offering.

I thought suddenly of my childhood home and how my mother would pick up any shiny thing off the sidewalk – a piece of glass or wire or wayward bracelet charm. How those things would find their way to the kitchen windowsill or living room mantelpiece, along with rocks and shells from beach vacations, feathers found out in the countryside. Once, playing in a dark corner of the basement, I had come across an artful scattering of shells on an abandoned shelf. Everywhere I turned were little arrangements, artifacts of life.

Finally Sugar examined my closet door. He stared into Guédé's face for a moment, then turned back to the bureau and grazed his fingers over a dusty pair of snake earrings from the dollar store.

"Nice." He turned to me with a small smile. "I see you."

***

Being possessed fascinates me. I like the idea of coalescence, merging the small self into a bigger whole. How sweet to transform the ego, to crack that hard little nut that guards its boundaries so carefully. To expand into something beyond the body or to be swallowed up by it, who can tell the difference?

I have read all kinds of accounts of Vodou ceremonies and what happens when spirits ride. There are things about it that frighten and attract me at the same time. The loss of control, for instance. When you are possessed you are literally out of your mind, and someone else is there.

Sometimes a spirit will punish a practitioner who has done wrong. I read an ethnologist's recollection in which Damballa mounted a man who had failed to properly serve him. Ridden by the snake spirit, the man effortlessly climbed a huge tree. When he was up beyond all reach of the congregation, Damballa departed, leaving him to figure out his own way down.

***

When he brought his face close to mine, my heart jumped and my whole body burned. He radiated heat and smelled like earth, cloves and something oily. I felt a little dizzy, and the silence around my head seemed to amplify my breath.

"You're open." He murmured. Our lips hardly touched as he breathed into me. An image of large, soft nostrils overpowered my mind, my first riding lesson suddenly resurfacing. Horses greet by breathing into each other's noses, I thought hazily. I was burning up. I sighed and he inhaled my exhalation. I floated to the bed, took off my shorts and lay down in my leotard, incapacitated by blood that felt too viscous in my veins. He shut the door behind him and removed his hat and several long beaded necklaces. He put these items down carefully in a pile, then stripped naked and shut my lamp off.

I watched him approach. From down on the bed, his darkened figure reminded me of the way shadows stretch long in evening sun. He eased onto me with his full weight, covering me like a blanket. Silky and leonine, heavy. He took my head and kissed my lips and cheeks. Then he was

61

beside me, shucking off my damp leotard. I opened up for him. Time and movement slowed and became dense. Honey replaced sand in the hourglass. I was being consumed by my own fire. I wondered when I would disintegrate, and would Sugar disappear too, or just find himself covered in soot?

Before either of us spontaneously combusted, he disentangled and pulled me to his side.

"That's enough for now," he told me. My face was hot and there were tears on my cheeks. I stared at him.

"I have to get back to the store," he explained. "And get ready for an event tomorrow." His mind was moving to the next thing; he gave me a small squeeze then got up and went into the bathroom. I heard the sink running. I tried to reconstruct what had just happened but the replay was already scratched and skipping. I was sweating again, my body agitated.

"It's me." He had come back in, was standing naked in front of Guédé. I sat up.

"With the teeth and everything," he continued. He mimicked the grin, pointing one finger at his own face and one at Guédé's.

It was true. Along with the usual accoutrement I had read descriptions of Guédé sporting, I had chosen to draw him with a funny gap-toothed grin akin to Sugar's.

"Who is this?" He asked.

"A Vodou spirit." I replied. He smiled and pulled his pants on.

"Wouldn't it make more sense to stay here and get some sleep, and go to the store in the morning?" I asked, trying not to plead. He shook his head, putting on his shirt.

"No, love. I really need to work on a few things."

He untangled the beaded necklaces and put them on one at a time, then tucked them under the shirt. I reached for him and he came to the side of the bed. I wrapped my arms around his waist, noticed his body was cool. He'd siphoned his fire into me. I looked up at him and felt inexplicably sad. He patted his pockets and came up with a small bottle.

"I have a solution," he told me, uncapping the bottle and taking out a dainty brush. He gracefully smudged a line of amber liquid on his palm and with ceremonial gravity, swept his hand over my pillow. It was earth, oil, and cloves.

"So that I can be here," he said. I wondered if it was a gesture of care or pity. He put on his hat and I walked him to the door. Then I came back and lay down with the pillow.

Logic told me a man is just a man, but my body could not be sure that I hadn't been hexed.

***

Riding my bike in an unfamiliar neighborhood one day, I got caught in a summer thunderstorm. When the rain let up to a drizzle, I decided I would walk the rest of the way home. Coming up a quiet side street, I saw Sugar's familiar figure approaching from the opposite direction across the street. A young girl was beside him, wearing his felt hat. When he caught sight of me, he took her hand and crossed to meet me.

"This is Angelia." He said, watching me carefully. A beautiful little girl. She had Sugar's eyes. She pushed the oversized hat up her forehead.

"Pleased to meet you," I said, and we shook hands. "Your daughter?" I asked him. He looked down at her, and I followed his gaze. Angelia smiled and nodded shyly.

"Her mom asked me to take her to a doctor's appointment. I'll talk to you later." He gave me a chaste kiss, and we all waved goodbye.

***

"Are you married?"

"No."

"Are you sure?"

"I promise."

"Were you ever married? To anyone?"

"No. Her mom and I weren't together like that."

"Why didn't you tell me you had a daughter earlier on?"

"What would you have done?"

"I don't know. But at least I would have understood."

"Understood what?"

"You. The situation I was getting into."

"I didn't know how to tell you. I'm sorry. Running into you like that was a relief."

We were both silent. Then I said, "It's hard now."

"What's hard?"

"I'm attached to you and I don't know if that's okay. Are you attached to me?"

"You chose me."

"What does that mean?"

"You chose me. I'm here for what you need."

"Nevermind. Talk to you later."

"Wait, hold on. I *am* attached to you." He said quietly. "But don't ask me to tell you that. Ask me to show you."

"Most people don't care for everyone they sleep with. The body can lie." I said.

"So can the mouth."

"I can't care for someone who's not open. It's too scary."

"Why?"

"Wouldn't you want to know who a person is and what they've got going in life? So you could make your own decision about it? I don't want to be sitting in the dark." He didn't respond. We were silent for a long time.

Finally, he said, "We're like soil and seed."

"What does that mean?"

"We're connected. And we're helping each other."

"How am I helping you?"

"You share a kind of...innocence with me. An openness."

"And what are you sharing with me?" I asked.

"The opposite." He said.

***

My apartment was on the ground floor and it sweltered in the heat of summer. Even with the windows open, no breeze blew in. Coming home from a long day of babysitting in someone else's un-air conditioned apartment, I sighed into the humidity. I had been neglecting D's class while I worked more to make rent, and my whole being was drained. I also felt slightly unhinged. I hadn't seen Sugar in two weeks, despite prayers for a chance encounter, a word from him. Any divine or magical intervention would do – some tangible sign of connection. I carried his presence constantly, but felt painfully uncertain as to whether he thought of me at all.

I went to the kitchen and looked at the refrigerator's bleak contents. A carton of almond milk, an ancient jar of olives. I went to the couch and sat, listening to fragments of street conversation, the rhythm of traffic. When the light changed I'd hear cars idling, lining up down the block. Sometimes a strange melody formed from many songs projected out of open windows. Other times there would be just one, which went flat and eerie driving away.

Abruptly overcome by fatigue, I went to my room to lie down. Late afternoon light angled in and I let it roast me. Kids from the daycare next door were playing outside. I listened to their voices; they shouted at each other like grown people. Then the voices faded as a teacher ushered them inside.

I groped for my phone on the mattress, thinking I would set an alarm in case I accidentally fell asleep. But I felt a form and realized Sugar had come in to lie down by me. My voice was gone, but he knew I was overjoyed. I closed my eyes and felt him shift onto me. I could barely breathe, my body magnificently heavy with his.

"That feels good." The words were hard to get out. He said nothing, but he crushed me, emanating love and warmth.

The sound of my own heavy breathing opened my eyes. I was alone, flat on my back in the oppressive heat of a sunbeam that had moved only slightly since I lay down. The feeling of the dream lingered, his presence so strong I almost believed that if I called out he would answer, emerge through the open door.

I found my phone and called, but he didn't pick up. I rolled to my side and closed my eyes. When my phone rang and roused me, the light through the window had gone from yellow to red.

"Hi there. Sorry I missed you."

"I just called to say you were in my dream." My voice was thick with sleep.

"A good dream?"

"Yeah. It seemed so real."

"What happened in it?"

"Nothing. But you felt close."

"I am close."

I glanced involuntarily at Guédé, staring and grinning from the closet door.

"I miss you." He said.

"Then why don't you reach out?"

"I am reaching out. I've been juggling all of my obligations."

"I'm not trying to be an obligation."

"I know, and I appreciate that. I'm going to come see you soon."

***

I went home in December to spend the holidays with my parents. It felt good to watch the city shrink down from the airplane window. I was relieved to find that all the volatile energy, life-and-death decisions and looming buildings were contained on a small island, that a world beyond New York still existed after all.

66

Getting home from the airport was an hour's drive through mostly empty countryside. My parents and I talked about life in the city and I elaborated on things I had told them over the phone; dancing, Vodou, the struggle to make rent. It was hard to summarize daily life with all its moving pieces and mystical occurrences waiting to unfold at any moment. They told me they worried about me, but that they were proud. I was overwhelmed; it seemed so long since I had received a straightforward statement of love. I had become accustomed to deciphering affection in Sugar's minimal, cryptic messages.

I was jetlagged and fell asleep before dinner. When I woke up it was a little after six in the morning, still dark outside. I tiptoed down the hall, past pieces of my mother's artwork that had hung for years in the same places, permanent fixtures in the landscape. I knew every creaky part, every dusty corner, every smell of the house as if it were part of my body. Downstairs, I put on my running shoes and slipped out. It took ten minutes to reach city limits, and I didn't encounter a single car, human or animal.

The stars were bright and sharp in the cold air; the eastern horizon was turning blue. I ran along a path heading towards the reservoir in the wheat fields beyond town. The fields were bare and tilled in preparation for warmer weather, when they would turn green and finally yellow-gold. I ran farther out, came to a long, steep incline and ran halfway up before I had to stop, winded. As my breath quieted, I became aware of deep silence; I heard nothing but my heartbeat. A pin prick of fear tingled in my spine. I had forgotten what absolute solitude felt like.

I took a moment to reason with myself, to ask why I was spooked if I was indeed by myself. Was it actually uncertainty as to whether I was alone? I saw nobody, no roaming farmer or coyote, yet my body was increasingly uneasy. I felt a strong urge to flee, so I began running again. I reached the top of the hill where the levy and trail joined – a beautiful view overlooking the reservoir, but I didn't slow down. I followed the path as it took me down, up, alongside farmers' fields and into groves of trees with naked, contorted branches. Still no other sign of life, yet I was neither looking for another presence nor running away from one that I knew about.

My lungs burned and my muscles began to fatigue. I had a sudden vision of myself as a bird might see me, a tiny figure moving almost imperceptibly through endless space. I slowed to a walk, my sweat instantly cooling.

Against the chill, I felt the heat and push of blood defining the borders of my body, speaking my aliveness. Still alone. I was calm again. I looked up and saw stars, the horizon's new pink and purple light.

***

"Are you coming back?" He asked.

"After the holidays."

"Will I see you?"

"You know the answer to that."

"It's nice to hear it."

"I can't distance myself from you."

"Because you chose me."

"Maybe. Did you choose me?"

"I let myself be chosen. By you."

"I hate when you say that." I said.

"Why? It's a statement about your power." I sighed in reply.

"I see you." He said.

"I know," I paused. "I hope our lives are always entangled."

"They will be. Who's in your room?" I glanced around my childhood bedroom, confused. Then I thought of Guédé, grinning into an empty room in Brooklyn.

***

The in-between and undefined is hard for me, and from what I've seen in the city it's hard for most people. I see the way we try to embrace mystery. We explore religion and spirituality, learn about planetary positions and meditation practices. But always with a purpose. To justify good or bad behavior, or to explain why so-and-so doesn't love us, or even to find a reason for keeping on, a story that makes sense enough that we continue struggling along the path to see what's next.

I struggled for a long time, searching for a narrative with Sugar. I desired clarity and began to write with the hope of finding it. A friend suggested that I'd never finish the writing until I reached some kind of conclusion with him in life. I thought she was right – I needed a resolution to understand the story.

Somehow, it's not so. If anything, I'm beginning to believe that no story ever has a resolution. There is always more string behind the loose end, and even when the whole thing comes unraveled there are still the remnants of what was, and what could be next. The curtain falls and the last page comes, but stories continue as long as life continues, and even death can't end them. A spirit clings, revealing itself in gestures, memories with no origin, lessons learned and words exchanged. Consciously or unconsciously, something keeps unfolding. It leaves its imprints.

David Smithson
Truman State University

Billi's Moment

Billi's mind slugged. She could barely lift her eyelids as she shoveled cereal into her mouth and gulped orange juice at her dining table in her small but pleasant apartment.

House plants littered every nook and cranny. Personal letters from friends and family were nailed to the white walls in haphazard places, spontaneous and free. The artwork could only be described as something from a flea market - quaint, charming, and cheap. It hung just as lazily as the letters, or else was found lounging in the chairs or leaning against walls and furniture.

Billi showed no interest in the suburbs she's lived in her whole life, or the people who lived there as they tried to play keeping up with the whoevers. She really, never displayed much direction in her life at all. Her wish though, if she could have one, would have been for some excitement.

Her eyes glazed over her possessions, her look conveying there was nothing on her mind but the sound of white noise marking each new day in Kingsley, Virginia. A suburb on the James River, its shores were littered with freighting ports that fed into the Atlantic. Her mind never quite realized the river as a pathway to the ocean and never really considered the ocean had other worlds on its sides.

When Billi snapped her car door shut, she jolted a bit from her seat. She reminded herself what she was doing.

"I'm going to work," she spoke it into the rearview mirror, winking sarcastically to herself. She drove off in her faded, tan 1996 Corsica through empty streets bathed in ambient street light. Fog enveloped everything in its sneaky chilled grasp.

Billi didn't mind her job as a night shift manager at Hultz'n Boltz gas station. Its location offered a view of the river, but only a sliver of water was visible during the day and none at all at night. The view was really of shipping ports, consisting of metal bars, winches, cranes, steel boxes painted either orange or blue, and rusted ships.

She never really resented the fact that all her talents were going to waste, even though she was quite unsure of where her talents lie. She could not, however, shake the thought that she was an imperceptible one of million with the same mundane experience, void of magic and surprise lurking around even a single corner.

After she had stocked the potato chips and the candy bars, Billi counted the cigarette packs, changed out the Dr. Pepper and Pepsi on the soda dispenser, mopped the floors, and plunged the men's restroom toilet. She never understood why they didn't make the opening of the male toilets bigger.

It was three in the morning by the time she could take a break. Business during this hour left Billi free to read the tabloids. Fake news was her favorite; she could at least be sure that it was indeed fake, filled with the most sensational stories.

Billi was highly engaged in a story out of Sentinel Butte, North Dakota, recounting the details of Brad Pitt's lurid vacation with Oprah Winfrey in the Badlands when a grey mass of bulbous flesh pulled the magazine out from her face.

An elephant stood on her freshly mopped floor. The slate color of the massive body clashed with the red and yellow theme of the station.

Billi dropped the article about Broprah's fervid love affair in stupification on the counter.

The elephant, a real and massive African dweller, filled the store. It was like an eclipse had snuck in through the front door without Billi even noticing, dimming the fluorescents around her.

The elephant towered over Billi.

Billi blinked, astonished and unbelieving. The elephant blinked lazily, unremarkably. Her extensive eyelids took a full three seconds longer than Billi's to shutter over her large brown-and-green-flecked eyes.

"Waazzzahowedanin," or something like that escaped Billi's mouth as her jaw hung open. Then, as if knowingly, the monster lifted its trunk in salutation.

At this conjecture, Billi couldn't be contained in her suspension of disbelief. She was fully aware that this was happening. She yelled at the top of her lungs, screaming that scream that only female vocal chords and Prince can produce. The sharp rise and impossibly-sustained note pelted through the quiet night. She held this until the elephant politely coughed.

"Would you kindly be quiet?" asked the elephant. She was indeed an elephant that could speak, which she continued to do so at some length. All the while stunned and petrified, Billi blinked along with the elephant's jovial movement. The elephant knocked over several packages of candy and lighters as she told her story about how she was smuggled on a cargo ship just three weeks ago by a man who called himself Burger from Angola, and how she had convinced him, somewhat forcefully, but obviously not life threateningly, that she needed to get to America.

"Well, I do think the particularities can be saved for another time, don't you? And how rude, I don't believe I introduced myself. My name is Wahn-di. It is a pleasure to make your acquaintance." The elephant said this with much fanfare, which was her way, bowing on the word "acquaintance," placing Billi back on her feet. For Billi had just a moment ago, during the latter part of Wahn-di's monologue, fainted ever so slightly and fell; now replacing her figurative jaw that reached the previously polished floor with her literal one.

Wahn-di waited patiently for a response, but then thought it better to probe the little human with a question.

"And what might your name be?"

Billi's mind was unfortunately being a tad stubborn, the cogs catching in the wheel while her eyes adjusted to the new brightness in the room after her spell.

As the human blinked mindlessly, the elephant made rounds about the store, making comments and asking questions. Since her decision to embark on a quest, Wahn-di had grown accustomed to dealing with humans and their perplexity in dealing with an elephant. She had discovered that these little creatures thought very highly of themselves; thinking that no other creature in the animal kingdom could dare match or, heaven's sake forbid, surpass the intellect of their own.

"What exactly is it that you do here?" asked Wahn-di.

Billi gave a squirm of the lips but uttered no sound.

"Hmmm, I see. Indeed. Prrr. Innn. Gelllss," Wahn-di pronounced, reading a tube's label.

"Preen-gulls," corrected Billi.

Wahn-di gave a look that belied intention before saying, "Oh, so it speaks?"

"Mmm," nodded Billi unintelligently.

"Not much though?" said Wahn-di, studying Billi. "Well that's quite alright."

"No. I talk. You know it is just that - well," Billi paused to look at her shoes, scuffing up the top of one with the bottom of the other, feeling nonplussed about her first words shared with a non-human.

"That I'm an elephant?"

"Well, yeah, it's that! Obviously," said Billi with a fit of grunting. "I mean," now Billi was coming to the realization of the situation she was in, and figured that she must be hallucinating or knocked herself from falling from the flimsy step ladder while trying to refill the soda machine. "I mean, I've never met a talking elephant!" Billi belted a great guffaw.

"Why are you laughing?" asked Wahn-di as she also began to giggle, mostly because of Billi's laugh. It was a great riot of a noise punctuated by deep silence.

"I don't know," hee-hawed Billi, her laughter continuing to build, forcing her to take great gasps between her words. "You - are - a - elephant."

"I - am - AN - elephant," Wahn-di said breathlessly in the midst of the hysterics. This little human entertained her a great deal.

"I can't breathe."

"Me neither."

"Wowza!"

"You said it!"

"Oh brother!"

"Oh sister!"

"Oww," exclaimed Wahn-di as she bumped her head on a long florescent light, sending it swinging.

"Oh dear." The laughter abruptly stopping. "Are you alright?" asked Billi.

"I'm fine," replied Wahn-di, massaging her scalp with her trunk. "I am curious, though, about what exactly it is you do here?"

"Well," began Billi, not quite on sure ground. "I - I am a manager at this, ah, gas-station."

"Mmm. And what is that, really?" asked Wahn-di.

"I make sure that all - well - you know, I make - and, you see, it's really simple in that I -"

But each false start of Billi's explanation made her think about how much her job felt futile and unimportant to the grand scheme of life; even to her own life it seemed remarkably trivial. How much she would give to have some sense of purpose. Shake off the shackles of the modern age. To just let go and run free. Billi couldn't quite come to an adequate explanation of the monotony of her occupation to this Serengeti woodland-dwelling creature.

Just then, the timer on an industrial coffee maker alerted the gas station of its finished process of brewing 98 ounces of Hultz-n-Boltz's "Ethiopian Excursion, with a mild nutty flavor." The alert spooked Wahn-di, causing her to knock over a kiosk of sunglasses with her great wide foot.

Wahn-di spluttered about, "Oh my, I'm dreadfully -." She stepped on about a dozen pairs all at once in her fluster. "My goodness, I'm so sorry darling," crushing another half a dozen. "My size in these compact areas - your species likes - can be quite disastrous at times, please -"

"No, no, no. Don't be-" Billi paused. She had an abrupt idea "That's my job!" she exclaimed.

"That's your job?" asked Wahn-di after several suspicious seconds.

"Yep," replied Billi, smiling broadly and sporting gusto. The look in her eyes was eating up her surroundings in delicious detail in her current state of epiphany.

Billi then heaved over a row of potato chips she had just stacked before

Wahn-di had arrived, the metal rack breaking against the floor. The bags of chips exploded their yellow, orange, and brown contents.

"Every night I come in and knock everything over and break whatever I can," explained Billi, punctuating her sentences with bouts of destruction. "And then - and then in the morning, a crew comes in and fixes it." She paused over a fallen rack of magazines, thinking. "Everybody knows it's pointless, but it's a way to give people work. Makes the politicians look good to show job growth." Billi paused again, hoping and praying the Elephant would buy it. "For the economy! Ya know?"

"No, I don't," said Wahn-di, giving the human a queer look.

"Right. Like I said everyone *knows* it's for show, but we do it all anyways because you need money in our society. But, I mean, that's really something we shouldn't worry about. What would be a lot of fun, and I'd probably get a bonus, is if you helped me out. I bet you can do a lot a damage real quick." Billi inspected the elephant, from her large toe-nails to the sprouts of thick black eyelashes that protected her emerald eyes, watching the great flowing ears wiggle ever so slightly before saying, "Whatya say!?"

"I see - so if I do this?" said Wahn-di as she ripped the light fixture out of the ceiling, the lights fluttering and raining large sparks on them both, scaring them in a way that was humorous just as soon as the fright dissolved.

"Yes!" yelled Billi, jumping onto the counter, reaching below to grab the baseball bat her boss put there for protection. Raising it above her head, she yelled like a banshee on the warpath, "LET FREEDOM RING!"

"INDEED!" Wahn-di joined the cry with a great bellow from her trunk before they both began their terror across the gas station.

Wahn-di sucked up all the hotdogs from the rotisserie, followed by the condiments from the dispensary, then she launched them like a potato gun, pelting the wall with splatters of ketchup, mustard, chunks of hotdog, all the while allowing her great mass to push over rack after rack of junk food.

Billi broke apart the cigarettes with great swings of the Louisville Slugger, sending them streaming through the air, tobacco falling like burnt confetti. She thought she was saving all the cowboys from lung disease.

Wahn-di sat on the large ice-cream freezer, crushing it all into one large rainbow sundae with a smash. She then added a few gas station bananas that she chewed-up and spit on top of the concoction of ice cream and metal. Burger from Angola, smuggler from her trans-global trek, had told her about ice cream sundaes, and now she was fully aware of what he meant by describing them as the best thing imaginable. She feasted on the new-found dessert, scooping gallons of ice cream into her mouth with her trunk.

Billi ripped open packs of water guns, filling them with ever flavor from the soda fountain, while Wahn-di ripped off each dispenser, allowing the contents to stream out in a fizzy river that flooded the floor. The two ran wild around the store soaking everything before breaking it. Billi with her super-soakers and baseball bat; Wahn-di with her trunk and vastness.

By the end of their rampage there wasn't a spot in the store that wasn't touched by their anarchy. Even that troublesome men's toilet was torn from its base and flung into the ATM, cash billowing from its broken deposit slit.

Billi sat on what was left of the counter puffing a corn-cob pipe filled with tobacco, blowing great clouds of smoke and the occasional smoke ring for fun.

"How'd you learn to do that?" asked Wahn-di, appreciating a delicate ring of smoke as it drifted over the gas-station carnage.

"My pops taught me," answered Billi, also regarding her handy work. "You try." Billi offered the pipe's end to Wahn-di.

Wahn-di inhaled the contents with her great trunk, nearly swallowing the entire pipe, and the embers burnt bright-red all the way to the bottom of the corn-cob's bowl. She then, wide-eyed and staring, let out a tremendous amount of smoke; they both laughed at the cloud as it engulfed them.

A few moments passed with serenity.

"Thanks so much," said Billi. "I really needed to do that - for some reason."

"You're welcome deary," said Wahn-di. "But next time, you don't have to lie to get me to have some well-deserved fun," winked Wahn-di.

"You knew!?"

"Of course! I may be an elephant, but I'm no Dumbo!"

Billi then noticed something curious, "Oh, oh dang, what is that!?" She was pointing with the end of her pipe towards a large something on the floor in the middle of the doorway.

"Oh that? Well…" Wahn-di sort of trailed off, rather shyly at first, but rushed forward in explanation instead, "I got dreadfully nervous, my dear, when the power flickered for that brief moment as you were messing with that electrical box. Sometimes I can be a bit skittish. And, well, you had worked me up so much, and we we're having such a good time. I didn't want to spoil it, you know, and I had already destroyed the toilets. And it has been an awfully long journey in a very confined space, I mean, really you couldn't expect me to just - truthfully I am typically a proper lady when it comes to matters of nature calling - "

Billi started to hee-haw again, but this time Wahn-di's cheeks flushed red.

"It's fine! Really!" exclaimed Billi after seeing Wahn-di's embarrassment. "I think it's magic! A work of art even." Billi blew another smoke ring.

"Yes," said Wahn-di, as she gave her excrement a side-eyed glance of unease. "As I said, it was a long journey…"

Billi felt empathy for the large lady, noticing perhaps for the first time just how beautiful the creature was, and how extravagant it was to have her here, particularly since she could somehow talk.

"Hey. Hey. Stop. Don't be embarrassed. Seriously, it's great!"

"Thank you," said Wahn-di, breaking off in a little shy giggle.

"Oh shoot," said Billi spotting a pair of headlights pulling up to one of the gas pumps. "We gotta get out of here quick!"

Wahn-di started for the front door.

"No, wait! If he sees you, we're screwed! We've gotta find another way. Shoot. He's coming," said Billi, noticing the man walking with his head down towards the gas-station. Billi and Wahn-di looked around frantically for an escape, but there wasn't one to be found. Wahn-di was simply too large.

"I will handle this," Wahn-di said with authority. The massive animal turned her entire figure around, bent her head forward toward the rear door, and bolted with all her might.

The crash created by the elephant was spectacular in effect and sound. The door absolutely flew. The concrete busted into a thousand pieces. The rebar was rent out towards the alleyway behind the station.

Billi stood flummoxed. Wahn-di stood immensely proud of herself, and a bit dizzy.

On the other side of the Hultz-n-Boltz, the man squinted and wondered what on earth had made the explosion. Not wanting to find out, he turned on his heels and re-entered his truck. *There are other gas stations in town*, he thought as he hurriedly sped away.

Regaining her senses, Billi followed Wahn-di as she trotted down the alley towards a vacant and well-lit road.

"Where in the world are you going?" huffed Billi, out of breath from trying to keep up with Wahn-di's long strides.

"I am headed to wherever my feet take me," responded Wahn-di.

"That's fantastic," said Billi. "But how exactly do you imagine you get there without being seen? I mean if someone sees you it could get ugly especially if you try to resist." Billi had an awful thought, "They could - could hurt you, or put you in a cage."

"I -"

Wahn-di halted in the middle of the amber alleyway next to a blue dumpster and a large black grease trap that did not smell pleasant in the slightest. A mouse was nosing across their path, lit by the buzzing light over the backdoor of Who Needs Vitamin D tanning salon.

"What are -" questioned Billi before noticing the mouse. "Oh, don't worry Wahn-di. I'll get rid of it."

Wahn-di held Billi back with her trunk.

"Please darling, do not disturb the little creature," said Wahn-di in a motherly tone. "It is only searching for food and shelter, and that is its sole concern."

"But aren't elephants deathly afraid of mice?" asked Billi.

Wahn-di threw back her head in a musically pleasing gaggle of laughter, capable of brightening up any old curmudgeon set in his ways.

"That is wonderfully delightful! Who assumed to tell you this lie, dear girl?" said Wahn-di as she wiped large jovial tears from her eyes with her elegant trunk.

"Well," started Billi somewhat embarrassed "I don't really - no one told me - I just - movies and - I don't know why I thought that."

Wahn-di focused on Billi with a look that, although void of pity, included a modicum of concern in her gaze. It was not of deep disturbed concern, but rather an acknowledgement of this fabled fact that had provoked the root of not only Billi's languishes, but the collective sigh of all mankind.

"In any case, I am not afraid of the mouse. I daresay that if he were to perceive us, as he would if we approached any closer, the poor creature's heart might cease to function from fright. No, I am simply allowing the little thing pass, to go on about its day, unmolested by what it might consider the most terrifying thing it has ever encountered - Me," said Wahn-di, who with an afterthought added, "and perhaps yourself."

The mouse whiskered its way to a large crumb of not-even-god-knows-what, bit into it, secured it in its mouth, then scuttled up the retaining wall that bordered the other side of the alleyway from the shops, scurrying out of sight.

"See," smiled Wahn-di, "that didn't take long now did it?"

"I guess not…" said Billi a little unsure of how to think about what had just happened. She thought it might be something big, but compared to everything else that had happened tonight Billi summed it up as a mere trifle in the end.

"But hey - look," pleaded Billi to the elephant. "It still goes without saying that if you continue to go along all laissez-faire like, you won't make it five miles from here."

"What do you suppose I should do?" Wahn-di asked as she turned her massive self to face the human.

Billi exhaled deeply before presenting her plan.

"Let me guide you. I'll use the map on my phone and see if we can't just cut through yards or parks or whatever, instead of walking down well-lit streets where you are bound to be spotted and then for sure caged or - worse." Billi paused looking into the dinner plate sized eyes of Wahn-di.

"Darling, thank you, but you may get into trouble. And what about your life -"

Billi cut off Wahn-di knowing what she was going to say. "I mean look," said Billi, calming herself down before continuing, "It isn't everyday - well *any* day, that someone gets to meet an elephant, let alone talk to one. And this, I mean - *this* - is everything I've been wishing. I mean hoping, that I could do with my life."

"What? Trek along with a talking elephant?" smiled Wahn-di.

"Yes. Well, no. Not really. I would have never dreamed of this! Never ever. But that's the point, isn't it? To do something in your life that when it happens to you, you don't know what to think, or even make of it. You just know that you gotta do it. So you do it!" Billi was beaming and looking up at the majestic creature, taking in all of her glory.

"Ya know?!" Billi finished hopefully and somewhat out of breath. So far, it had been a very tiresome, albeit extraordinary morning.

"Yeah. I suppose I do," the elephant winked.

Billi turned from the bright street that lay ahead to the darkness masking the way they had come, where not a single light flickered, almost blank in its depiction.

"So, what now?" asked Wahn-di

"Follow me," said Billi.

Adam Virzi
New York University

Funny Money

Two suits leaned over neat whiskey. The bartender stood off to the side pretending not to hear.

"Anything can happen on a business trip to New York. Why this?"

"Because ordinary business is about making money. This is about how we use it." The larger of the two finished off his whiskey. He pulled his head right, stretching the veins that protruded from his thick neck, and called the bartender over with a single well-manicured finger. He waited for his glass to be filled before continuing. "We have nothing to worry about. We're here every other week, the room was paid for in cash for four days, and by Sunday we'll be gone without a trace."

"It's just so – so pointless." The second man's frame trembled from the weight of his glass. His scrunched face led to the tip of his nose, which seemed to search the air for words to describe his situation that had gone too far.

"They're the ones that are pointless."

"B-but how do you not think of them as… " The large man's glare seemed to read the small man's words, as if written whispers in the air. Scrutiny diminished his voice to a mere squeak, "…people?"

"You worked for years to make a name for yourself. You had to do some not-so-nice-stuff to accomplish that, but I helped you every step of the way. Have I led you astray yet?"

"No. I mean – I don't know."

"That's right. All that's left is proving to yourself that it was worth it."

"I've bought everything I've ever wanted. What more is there to prove?"

"Petty proof of privilege. What's your proof of power?"

"This."

Without reply, the large man drained his glass. Shaking off the burn with a grin, he tapped the smaller man on the lapel of his suit, expelling air through the trumpet of a pocket square, and called him along with a finger, as he strode away from the bar.

After chugging against the sloshing of whiskey in his glass, the smaller man fumbled with a wad of bills and tossed them on the bar.

When they had gone, the bartender bused their glasses from the dark mahogany. He picked up five one hundred-dollar bills and, upon examining them, was happy to not have heard.

***

Two king beds did not fill even half of the spacious room. The larger man sat on the edge of one bed with his back to the drawn blinds. His eyes were lost in the red flames licking off the canvas painting on the wall. Arms rested on his thighs, he repeatedly clenched his right hand into a fist, releasing it only to roll his wrist and restrain the skin over his red-white knuckles.

The toilet flushed behind the bathroom door. A man stepped out of the bathroom wiping the water left onto his hands upon his face, dirt-stained droplets trickling into his nettled beard. He was gaunt, the muscles in his arms thinned and strung to his bones like worn out rubber bands. Massaging the crooks of his elbows seemed to be more reflex than choice. He smelled like you would expect a homeless junkie to smell: a combination of cold sweats like sour milk and festering urine. One suspected much of the smell was trapped in the wild knots conjoining the matted hair on his head to beard.

The junkie lowered himself cautiously onto the bed opposite the rich man. The tension in his knees filled the room with the edge that a creaky mattress might lend to less expensive accommodations. But it had to be a slow recline, should the mattress's plush cushioning decide to reject his brittle bones so used to the learned firm comfort of cardboard boxes.

He looked at the rich man who had brought him here. The man's glare seemed to lance right through him, preferring instead to look at nothing at all. Used to such dejection, the junkie's eyes drank in the elaborate furnishings of room. The poor son of a bitch didn't think twice about the painful, angry silence in the room like black curtains drying on lines of tension strung throughout the air. He just sat there letting the rich

82

man's disgusted glare run him through.

The room's door opened. The small rich man slipped through the first opening, and once ajar there stood in the hall outside the room an old bum. He wore filthy green sweatpants and a broken-in Yankees cap. His yolk-yellowed eyes scanned the room before stepping over the threshold. The smaller man closed the door behind him.

"Who are these people?" He asked the man who had brought him here.

"Of all the trash on the street, this is what you pick up?" The large man said to his friend.

"Pick me for what?" He refused to be silenced.

"Are you shitting me, Saltz? If you didn't tell him why he's here this is sure going to be interesting."

"Why don't *you* tell me why I'm here, then?"

"Would you shut the fuck up?" The large man screamed. The veins in his neck bulged and his eyes flared red. "For God's sake, people are talking here."

"I'm minding my own business and this funny little white guy come up to me saying come get cleaned up, have a bite to eat. I knew that shit was too good to be true, but this shit wasn't even worth leaving the street for." The bum turned to leave.

The large man swallowed his spite, "If you stay, it could be more than worth your while." Spitting avarice at the poor seemed to come more naturally to him.

"I'm listening'"

"Fifty grand."

"What for?"

"Ending this pathetic excuse for life." The large man acknowledged the junkie's presence for the first time after entering the hotel.

"This some fucked up shit."

"Don't think you have it in you, or can you just not imagine yourself with so much money?" The bum eyed the large rich man. "The only ones who kill with impunity are the rich, but the only ones that are killed without a trace are the poor. Together we're the perfect crime."

The bum shook his head and turned to leave. After two steps toward the door, the junkie had dredged himself from the depths of the mattress. After three, the junkie was on his back, teeth sunk into the collared slope of his neck. Hunching under the weight, the bum threw the junkie forward into the wall, where he fell to the floor with a thud heavier than one would expect from such a hollow body.

The bum backed toward the door. Hand reaching out behind him, he searched for the latch, watching as the junkie rose and reared for another attack. Hand grasped handle. It turned, and as the bum spun to exit, the junkie tackled him up against the door, slamming it shut and cracking the back of the bum's head against the solid frame. Recoiling off the wall, the bum drove the junkie forward, their joined momentum spilling over the edge of the bed and onto the mattress. Wrestling wrists, the junkie reached up from beneath the bum's weight, arms driven by strangling addiction in an attempt to wring the life from him. Despite old age and a broken body, the bum easily reached through the junkie's flailing arms to reach his neck. He felt a dull pulse from the carotid artery, slowly surrendering.

The bum closed his eyes in order to let the good in him escape so the ugly could do what it needed to survive.

His eyes opened, and his clenched hands released the neck long enough to shift into a tight grip around the base of the junkie's skull. The bum lifted the junkie's head like an impossibly heavy stone, and without compromising a point in fluid motion, brought it down as heavily on the angled corner of the night stand. The edge sliced through skin and wedged into the back of the junkie's skull. The tension straining the muscles in the junkie's arms snapped and they fell limply to his sides.

***

The large rich man's heavy hands punctuated the silence of the room in loud, drawn out claps.

"I must say. That was more than I could have asked for fifty grand." He reached into his pocket.

84

"You better shut yo' ass up." The bum spewed a fury of curses on the rich man, biting his cracked black lips on the 'f' of his profanity and clenching his eyes in rage before layering it on. "I'm living life the best way I know how, which, turns out, hasn't been great at all. But I know my place, and from it, I see shit you couldn't possibly see from inside your little bubble. I'm not gone bother educating you, motherfucker, because to the people whose lives you're stepping into with bloody shoes, this shit ain't funny. I don't know how many times you done this evil, but you better believe this'll be your last. Making sure of that is about the only decent deed I've got left to choose from."

"Oh, stop your whining. What do you want, twice as much? Triple?"

"I don't want your dirty money. I want…"

The rich man slapped the bum across the face. The sting on his cheek was recognition enough that the rich man heard exactly what he said. As the emptiness within the bum filled with a rage unfelt since a youth spent cutting his teeth on the streets, he readied himself to fight.

Blinded by fury, the rich man leaned into a punch aimed at the bum's face. Stepping left, the bum drove his scarred knuckles into the man's strong jaw, shattering the bones up through to his sharp cheekbone. The rich man hit the floor. Without moving his neck, he spit several jagged flints of whitened tooth out with a thick string of blood. He picked himself up, dazed by impact, and was caught by a pummeling of fists working his kidneys and liver, paying sufficient attention to the ear, and finally giving due attention to the unbroken mask covering half of the rich man's true face.

The rich man crumpled to the ground and began to crawl backwards, away from the bum. Standing over the rich man, the bum watched hot tears fall from the man's bloodshot eyes as he wiped blood away from his now unrecognizable face. The bum went to the mini fridge and found a half bottle of vodka. He walked back over to the rich man and poured several shots over the fresh cuts around the man's eyes. Devilish screams poured from the rich man's depths. Pressing his hand down on the imploded bridge of the man's fractured nose, the bum slicked away the vodka-mixed blood enough so that the man could see. Looking up with burned, blurry sight, he saw the bum raise the bottle to his lips, draining it of its last fourth, bend down on one knee, lift the bottle above his head, and bring it down like the hand of God on the Earth's mightiest sinners.

The bum smashed the bottle into the rich man's face until there was none of it left. The sole exception was a faint and infrequent bubbling of blood from where the mouth must have been. That, too, died out.

Squeaking from the corner of the room betrayed the smaller rich man. The bum walked over to the man directly responsible for involving him in this gore. So much rage had been exorcised on the room's most-recently deceased, the bum was able to see that killing this pitiful soul wouldn't do anything to alleviate his own guilt. But it would; it would ensure that this particular brand of guilt was never again inflicted on another human being.

The rich man cowered behind raised knees and open palms. The bum kicked each of his limbs back from the body so that the man was spread out on the floor before him. Raising his soleless shoe, he brought his heel down sharply on the rich man's neck, crushing the windpipe and giving rise to a geyser of blood. A desperate gasping for air, accompanied by the scratching of hands grasping for something, anything that might stifle the loss of life, filled the silence of the room. The bum kicked the man's hand away from his throat and stepped on it firmly as to crush all the bones in the fingers and palms. The man reached for the bum's leg and sunk his claws into ankle. That hand received an even worse torture, which brought the rich man over the brink of consciousness.

**

The bum stumbled back from the body. The good in him returned to find the ugly quite drunk, in the midst of a triple homicide, his guilt for which was marked upon his skin by a sheen of sweat and blood. Silencing the first of what would be many sobs, he broke down in tears.

Staggering into the bathroom, the bum fumbled with the shower knobs until steam began to cloud the mirrors. His dirty clothes, now ruined by blood, rested on the tile floor. The man, naked before himself and God, cried repentance under the searing water. Blood and sweat mixed with the beads wicking down his body and made its way to the drain. Next, the water washed the grit accumulated in the finest traces of his skin since his last shower. Finally, the water washed over the fault lines in his body. Some were new, irreparable fissures from the guilt of blood on one's hand. Some were old, the stresses, aches, and pains from a life exposed to the elements of an unforgiving city.

He stepped out of the shower baptized a murderer. He wiped the fog from the mirror over the sink and looked at the image of himself before tragedy. One could not see the physical marks of murder. Those resided in his sunken eyes and in the muscles of his hands. But he was no longer comfortable with the image of his old self. Finding everything he needed to change that laying on the sink, he began to reconstruct himself in the rich image of evil he had come to know. He ran hair clippers close over his scalp. He tugged a razor against the thick coils of hair on his face. Running water from the sink consecrated the transformation.

The bum exited the bathroom, finding clothes in the dresser. A new pair of socks stretched over his feet. The elasticity of clean underwear was tight on his hips. The hug of a pure white undershirt provided the closest thing to an embrace he had known in years. He found pressed slacks and an expensive cotton shirt, which the dulled coordination of his knobby fingers struggled to button. In the closet by the door there were several suit jackets. Pulling one from a hanger and slipping in, it immediately bespoke the dimensions of the large rich man. It was a good fit, but felt like a false skin. He walked over to the large man's body and removed his shoes. The patent leather stretched around his feet. He looked in the mirror on the opposite wall and saw nothing but a drunken bum dressed in a rich man's clothing.

You can dress up a bum in designer clothes but he isn't rich until his pockets are full. Searching both of the dead rich men turned up the promised fifty grand, eight stacks of hundred dollar bills. Four fit perfectly in each deep pocket.

As the bum took the Do Not Disturb sign from the inside door handle, several feeble words floated on faint but forced rasps of breath to form a broken sentence.

"Please. Don't leave. Me. To die."

He looked down at the small rich man, who wouldn't be drained entirely of life for many hours, maybe days. "I couldn't take any chances with your friend. But you – I want you to lay here and suffer until someone finds you rotting. By that time come I'll have taken this money here and done my best to put it in pockets where it'll be spent to bring life, not death."

The bum walked out into the hall. Closing the door behind him silenced the quiet cries of the dying man inside. He placed the Do Not Disturb sign on the outside of the handle and walked away.

***

The elevator doors slid open. Tightly laced patent leather shoes stepped out onto the rich crimson carpet. All the eyes in the lobby turned to him for a moment before returning to their own business. The bum's feet still felt strange in the rich man's shoes. As he walked toward the exit, a terrible fear of the outside world came over him and he ducked into the hotel bar for fortification.

The bartender stood off to the side cutting lemons. When the bum sat down, he looked up briefly before returning to work. After scanning the bottles of whiskey on the top-self, the bum cleared his throat to call the bartender away from his paring knife once again.

"The bottle on the top right. No, one more over. That one. Fill me up a glass of that."

"It's forty-eight dollars a shot."

"Oh yeah," the bum said. He remembered the money in his pocket and removed one of the eight stacks. Seeing the cash, the bartender stopped him from fumbling through the bills and asked if he would like to open a tab.

The bartender placed the glass on a crisp white napkin in front of the bum and stepped back to stand with his hands folded in front of him. The drink called the bum's attention away from the stack, the open end of which he had been flipping through, enjoying the rich sensation on his fingertips. He knew how dangerous it was to go from having nothing to sitting at a bar, his concentration kept from drinking by the titillating brush of crisp hundred-dollar bills fanning ones fingers. He replaced the money, knowing that the rich men dead ten floors above had made that change in a much longer and harder climb.

The bum picked up the glass. He took a small sip, leaving his nose in the aromatic thick of dark honey, marzipan, and malt, and, without lowering the glass, tipped back its remains. As the taste aged on his pallet he closed his eyes. He would need to remember this taste for the dark days to come. While his eyes were closed to take in the full sensory experience of rich man's whiskey, his hand had somehow found its way back into his pocket. Without releasing his clutch he withdrew all four stacks and placed them on the bar in front of him.

"Anything else for you sir?" The bartender was eager to please.

"Another one of those. And a pen if you have one."

With both in front of him, the bum reached first for the whiskey. After a long draw he replaced it on the bar. He wanted to look closely at the money. He had only ever seen a hundred dollar bill a few times in his life, and he had never *really* looked at one before. It took mouthfuls of whiskey for him to puzzle out how something as simple as dyed cloth could have so much power over people's lives. He wanted nothing more than to be able to pick up the pen and cancel out that power the way he would be able to do with any other printed symbol. But it wasn't really the symbols printed on the bill that made it powerful. It was the bill itself. No amount of ink could cover up or alter what that symbol stood for.

He took the pen in his hand. Writing slowly and deliberately he printed the first words that came to mind over the face of Benjamin Franklin.

CIRCULATION IS THE SYMPTOM

OF A HEALTHY ECONOMY.

WHEN MONEY ONLY MOVES UP

BILLS AREN'T BROKEN,

CHANGE ISN'T MADE.

He leaned back to read what he wrote. Then he finished off his drink and pushed the glass forward, begging for another serving.

The bartender looked uneasy, as if personally offended by the desecration of a symbol he held above all others. "Sir, I – I won't be able to accept marked bills."

The bum frowned. Sizing up the unmarked stack in front of him, he decided that he must make every bill there count. So he reached into his pocket and removed six hundred dollars of the money he set aside for himself.

"Keep the change. Just keep these coming 'til I'm done or the bottle finished."

The bum leaned over the four stacks of money and began to copy out the same message on every last bill. Every fifty or so bills he would take a sip of whiskey. Every hundred he'd make sure he was finished with the glass. Eventually his hand began to hurt so badly that he needed to increase the pace of his drinking in order to alleviate the cramping that comes from not writing a single word for over ten years.

When the final word was printed, he dropped the pen and stood, stool legs scraping against bar floor. Too drunk for formalities, he drained the remainder of his glass and stumbled out of the bar, past the hotel reception, and onto the street from which he came.

***

The bum closed out the day by traveling to the far reaches of the city in search of New York's homeless – the unseen, the downtrodden, the dispossessed. He found solitary men, mad women, helpless children, and families huddled together on the street. To each he gave a hundred dollar bill. When asked how he could be thanked he gave the only response that his whiskey-soaked brain could formulate: pay as much of it forward as you can without paying it up.

The bum didn't know how the money would be spent. All he knew was that twenty-five thousand dollars had just entered the free market. The only marks it bore attaching it to the tragedy he had suffered was the message he had been saving up inside for an opportunity where someone might find incentive to listen. Of course the money would make its way to back up to the top one percent. All money does eventually. That was the point. His only hope was that on its way up it would trade hands enough to make a difference.

***

By the time he divested himself of the last hundred dollars, the liquor had set him to stupor. He woke up in a blur without clothes, the patterns of cold concrete pressed into his stiff and broken body. The dry cracking of a blood-painted upper lip led him to discover a broken nose. He must have been jumped. It serves him right for handing out money to the poor, doesn't it?

Whoever jumped him must have wanted to make sure he'd

remember. They beat him beyond senseless. Stripping him and leaving him exposed wasn't dehumanizing enough. They wanted to make an object for humiliation out of him. One other people could enjoy. Little did they know that he already was.

***

The bum crawled from the alley to the busy street.

"Dollar for a joke?" he called out to the passerby. His voice fell on willfully deaf ears, "Who wants to hear a joke?" Those who looked snickered and kept walking.

Frederick Tran
University of Texas- Arlington

Airstrikes

"We're running low on supplies," Marc half-whispered in French.

"I'm sure the trucks are on their way. Probably held up at some checkpoint on the other side of the city. Last shipment took six weeks to get here," I gurgled from around my toothbrush. I spat the toothpaste into the sink, unsure why he was whispering. We weren't at the hospital around patients and our only neighbors lived two buildings over. Our only roommate, Mona, was dead asleep on her bed when we got home from the hospital today.

"It'll be too late. Most of these children need food now; otherwise they'll die." He leaned against the brown stucco in his dirty green scrubs as he waited for my response.

"What's your point?" I asked, suddenly feeling the weight of exhaustion hit me. I was in no mood to argue in circles with him – especially tonight.

"Is there one? We are wasting our medical supplies and dwindling water on people who won't survive once they leave this hospital." We switched spots; I sat down cross-legged next to the sink and Marc took his turn to brush his teeth.

"So they won't," I replied, pulling my brown hair up into a bun. I'd wash it in another two days – it didn't smell too terribly yet and we were trying to conserve the water we had left. I peeled off my scrub top and decided to leave the white tank top on. I was too tired to change tonight.

"Are you saying we let them stay?" Marc asked incredulously, his mouth filled with toothpaste foam. Under different circumstances, I probably would have laughed. He looked so funny- this talented surgeon letting foam drip from his mouth onto his week-old scrubs with his untamed black hair and raised eyebrows. He had become a stark contrast from the well-dressed man I met years ago in medical school, before we made the decision to serve in Yemen.

Time had suited him well. He had filled out his tall and lanky frame. A substantial amount of silver hairs began to mix in with the raven black. The crow's feet didn't do much to hide his exhaustion. We were all exhausted.

92

Marc, Mona, and I were some of the volunteers that Médecins Sans Frontières had sent to here. Mona, a British midwife, had been here much longer than either of us. She had the pleasure of watching the last OBGYN specialist pack his bags and leave four months before we arrived. Marc was a trauma surgeon from France and I a Swiss pediatric surgeon. We did not have a difficult time getting placed, especially with our high proficiency in French and our willingness to pick up Arabic.

Getting into Yemen, however, was a difficult task. The rebels had taken over the airport, but the airspace was still controlled by the Yemen government. The only way there was via a small private plane from Djibouti – no commercial airline had flown into the area in years.

The drive to Taiz from Sana'a was just a brief glimpse into what the Yemenis have dealt with for the past several years. Numerous checkpoints held us up from several minutes to several hours due to frequent searches for weapons and ammunition. Many of the bridges have been completely obliterated, leaving us no choice but to drive down through the wadis. The dry riverbeds provided a mostly smooth surface to drive across, giving us perspective to the severe water crisis undergoing the country. The car engine stalled going up the incline. Marc, the guide, and I had to push the car up before we could move on to the next checkpoint.

"We can't send them to die," I snapped, fiddling with the gold ring on my necklace. The three of us had just completed a three-day shift at one of the six remaining hospitals in the city. Marc and I had spent the past 24 hours patching up four boys with the hospital director, who was the only Yemen surgeon left in that part of the city. The boys had been playing wallball with a UXO. They had lobbed the grenade at the wall until it exploded, leaving one dead, two severely injured, and one with superficial wounds. They couldn't have been older than eight. Hassan, the hospital director, and I operated in the first boy with our makeshift tools and diminishing medical supplies for most of the day – we had to amputate because there wasn't any salvageable tissue in the boy's leg. Marc spent half the day removing shrapnel from the second boy and suturing the third.

"We can't let them stay at the hospital either. There's not enough staff or space to tend to them all. There's definitely not enough supplies to keep them and take on new patients Julie." He began to strip out of his hospital scrubs. My eyes lingered on the matching gold ring in a bigger size on his necklace.

"What are you saying?" I realized that this wasn't about the patients. He folded his arms over his chest, leaning on the opposite wall. His face said it all before he even replied.

"Maybe it's time," he admitted quietly.

I was disinclined to continue this conversation with him. I got up, suddenly awake from the irritation I felt, and walked into the room that Mona and I shared.

I lay awake in bed that night, clutching the faded gray blanket in my hands like a lifeline. The roar of the airplanes from above signaled the beginning of the airstrikes. The whistling of the falling bombs was followed by the echoing drums of war. No matter how many times I had braced myself, nothing fully prepared me for the intensity that ripped through my bones as bombs exploded at nearby buildings. The ceiling sprinkled another layer of dust onto the barely furnished room. I could see the still outline of Mona huddled beneath her blanket in the twin bed opposite mine. I never understood how she managed to sleep through the bombings – I suppose she had grown numb to the feeling and noises after spending nearly a year here. By staying awake, all we really could do is pray that the bomb didn't hit our house and hope that our neighbors would be alive tomorrow.

We left the next morning in a car as cold and silent as a grave. Mona had picked up on the tension between Marc and me and opted to sit in the front while Marc drove. The silence outside could have fooled anyone into believing that the city wasn't currently tearing itself apart. Marc drove slowly through the barricaded streets, hoping that the slow crawl wouldn't disturb the slumber of war.

It was almost startling how stark the contrast was between two adjacent streets. One could be completely devoid of any form of life; the only reminders were leftover barricades and rubble from destroyed businesses and homes. Turn the corner and it was a whole new world. Suddenly, people wandered from the confines of their homes to the open market stalls on the side of the road. Children played games in the empty spaces outside to pass the time. But nothing was untouched by the war. The prices of the ware in the market stalls had surged from the embargo. The children's new favorite pastime was named "one-two-three airstrike" where they flung themselves to the ground. Morbid humor was all they knew.

The hospital itself had altered greatly since our arrival. The number of beds had tripled and the intensive unit was forced to expand in order to accommodate the amount of dying patients who arrived every day. But even those weren't enough when the airstrikes began.

Mass casualty occurred so often here in Taiz with the ever-changing frontlines. The medical tents we set up outside had become permanent fixtures of the hospital. Even triage worked differently out here. Many of the patients who were able to come were often labeled with black bracelets, meaning all we could do was attempt to offer them some comfort before they passed. Red represented patients who required immediate surgery or treatment, yellow for the injuries or illnesses that could wait up to twelve hours, and green for the patients who could still walk without any assistance.

Mona headed up to the second floor to the Mother and Child unit. She was caring for the hospital's first neonatal twins. She had been forced to create a makeshift baby warmer out of a heat lamp. Marc and I hurried in to prepare for the onslaught of our next shift. Stethoscope around my neck, I pulled back the curtain of the first room on my rounds and found a frantic mother pacing in the small space.

"What's wrong?" I asked her softly in Arabic.

She stopped her pacing and gestured frantically towards her crying baby. "I don't know. He has diarrhea and vomiting," the mother told me, desperation leaking from her brown eyes. "It doesn't stop. I can't make it stop."

I checked him over. I could count his ribs without close examination. His chapped lips immediately confirmed what I found in many patients. His skin was a sickly yellow, matching the bracelet he wore. I was sure that under her baggy black gown, I would have found a similar situation.

"I think he's severely dehydrated, nothing some water wouldn't fix, inshallah." I jotted a note down and handed it to her. "The nurse out front should be able to get you some supplies."

She managed to shoot me a watery smile when I handed her the note, but I watched it quickly fade away.

"I don't know how to get home," she admitted to me sadly. She picked up her baby and began to try to soothe his pain away. "My husband and I paid 15000 Yemeni Rial to get here and it'll cost that much to get back."

Such was the life for those who made it to our hospital. Some of the patients we received paid with nearly everything they had because they lived too far to walk with their conditions or injuries. Often times, they didn't have the money to make it back to their homes. The problem, as Marc had pointed out, was that the hospital had neither the space nor resources to keep old patients and see new cases.

I rounded on a patient we had admitted several days prior, a little boy named Salem. One of his neighbors had gone into the burning building after a bomb had fallen to pull him and his mother out from the flames and rubble.

"Ummi?" the toddler questioned me in Arabic, looking at me with pleading eyes. Despite the hundreds of patients I have cared for since my arrival, I didn't know how to break the news to the little boy that his mother was dead.

I had seen her. Marc and some of the nurses had tried to ease her suffering, but death came slowly for her. She was covered in third degree burns – her selfless sacrifice to save her son's life after she threw herself over him to shield him from the falling mortars. Despite a war ravaging around them, a family in Yemen was no different from any other family around the world. What mother doesn't have the urge to protect her child?

Though I had spent the better part of two months here treating patients, I was unprepared for the injuries sustained by a teenage girl after the strikes last night. I'd never seen anything like it, not even in medical textbooks or journals. Half of her body had been torn from her, yet she was still awake and responsive. She begged me to stop the pain. Marc and I paired up to try to save her life in surgery, despite knowing that the odds were heavily stacked against us. A body without a pelvis or limbs could not survive, yet here she was. The least we could do was try.

But the miracle ended there. The surgery was futile. We tried to numb some of her pain and moved her into a bed in the intensive care unit. Marc opted to take a smoke break on the roof and I followed. Since coming here, Marc rarely smoked since cigarettes were a luxury item and the ones he had smuggled in were in limited quantity. We had only smoked together twice before today – both when we worked together on a difficult case where we lost the patient despite our best efforts.

Marc lit the cigarette and took the first drag. He passed to me and I welcomed the warm smoke into my lungs. I rested my head on his shoulder as we passed it. The tension in the air eased as we both relaxed into each other. Our legs dangled over the edge of the roof. I took in the view as we sat in comfortable silence. Despite the horrors we had seen, the clear blue sky proved that there was always beauty left in the world if you looked hard enough.

"I think you're right," I finally admitted, breaking the silence. His arm rested comfortably around my waist. He took the last drag and flicked the butt behind us.

"About what?" He exhaled.

"I think it's time we go home." I shifted to catch his intense gaze. His eyes scanned my face and I could feel relief wash over him. We both leaned in and shared a kiss. Our teeth clacked together but none of the awkwardness mattered. He broke the kiss when we heard the roar of incoming trucks and I continued to hold my head in his hands.

"I can't wait to marry you," he whispered as we sat with our foreheads pressed together. The door to the roof burst open and a giddy Mona ran to the edge.

"Grâce à Dieu! The supply trucks have finally come," she shouted excitedly, waving her arms in the direction of the trucks. The world came rushing back in and we all watched for them to appear in view. We cheered when they finally did, rushing back inside to meet them on the ground level. The feeling of excitement grew throughout the hospital as news spread from both personnel to patients. The happy chatter almost drowned out the sound of an airplane flying over.

The shockwave from the explosion ripped through me. I felt as though someone had taken a sledgehammer to every part of my body and jammed icepicks into my ears. My jaw instinctively clamped shut, as if fastened with a sharp twist and tighten of a screwdriver. With every explosion, the earth shook and all I could do was hold on to myself. My ears rang as I choked on dust and plaster. The blasts continued and I merely laid there, my head in my arms, trying to shield myself from falling debris. Thick white smoke filled the air. As quickly as the attack began, it was over.

I coughed and pushed the ceiling debris off of me. I continued to sputter and cough out all the chalky dust that had made its way into my lungs as I stood up. I immediately felt vertigo and blood began to pour down my face when I finally got to a standing position.

Merde. I touched my forehead and winced. That was going to need stiches. I wiped my hand on the side of my scrub top and winced. My ribs were probably bruised or broken, but it hurt too much for me to actually try to check. The thick smoke made it hard to see if anyone else survived and I could feel panic bubble in my chest.

"Marc?" I hoarsely called out. "Marc!" It was beginning to get difficult to distinguish if the ringing in my ears was from the aftershock or if it was screaming from the chaos around me.

I took a step and the ringing seemed to intensify. I looked down and saw a familiar hand. A hand that caressed my face just minutes ago, which could have been an eon ago.

"Marc!" I cried out. I began to move the smaller pieces of rubble off of his body. The larger things were harder to move, but I gritted my teeth and pushed through the pain. Finally shoving them off him, I fell to my knees and began to shake his still form.

"Marc. Marc. Please, God no." I begged as I continued to try to stir him awake. I pounded on his chest and watched the golden ring bounce on his bloodstained shirt before falling still. I grasped his mangled hand in mine as I pressed kisses to it, wishing that each one would somehow do the impossible. The broken bones I felt as I pressed his hand to my chest only reaffirmed what I already knew.

My vision began to blur as tears cleaned my cheeks of the white powder and blood. I felt Marc's body shift and Salem crawled out from under. Bitter resentment filled my bones as the boy threw his tiny, dust covered arms around my neck.

"Ummi," I felt him whimper sadly into my collarbone. My arms moved of their own accord as they wrapped themselves around the boy. I felt no pain as numbness began to set in. I looked up to the missing ceiling to see the blue sky. The thin tendrils of white floated across the sky as the sun illuminated the settling dust around me, covering the ruins in a soft blanket of white.

When they removed Salem from me, I let them. I didn't protest despite his desperate cries. I never wanted to see him again. His face was a constant reminder of the body bag I laid next to. But when I was strapped to a spinal board, I wondered what Marc would have done if I had been the one to sacrifice my life for Salem's. Would he have left a little boy to a hopeless future? I tried to swallow the lump in my throat. The two rings on my chest felt like a heavy anchor and I allowed it to pull me into the darkness.

One, two, three, airstrike.

Margaret Koger
Boise State University

Handy Girl

After I slip on my nightie and brush my pearlies, I swish over to the mini-kitchen and pretend I'm leaving my hands on the counter. It eases my mind a little to remember what it was like before. In the mornings it I'd jiggle those plastic gizmos back on my stubs, latch the Velcro, and turn the heat up on the water for coffee. I guess people who say love is on the flip side of hate know what's what, and sometimes … well, I can't believe he's skipping out on me now after he hung in there all the time I struggled with my fakies.

After the honeymoon, I'd gotten into the habit of hand pouring hot water onto a filter full of fresh ground because Seth hated hearing coffeemakers doing their drip, drip, drip thing. When he was here, I loved to watch him fill the kettle at night, counting out four cups of cold water – two for each of us. These days I just set the timer on automatic before I go to bed. Who'd have ever thought things would turn out this way?

"Why leave now?" I asked when he started packing up.

"Your new hands are creepy, Janie. You don't know how they twitch and crawl in the night – I can't sleep, and I – what the hell, eh?" Then he slammed out the door and the last of my illusions winked out like a batch of dying stars.

Seth gave me hope for a life kind of like everybody else had – even with those artificial hands. And now? Creepy old circus-style sideshow weird. Step right up ladies and gents! Life should go: baby, kid, teen, grown-up, and gray hair. I'm barely into my twenties and I can tell it's my last act. Only me onstage and the curtains coming down. I started out *normal* (until the accident), then hit *recovery* (prosthetics), and now *freak* (transplant) – a sad show all around.

Back when I was a teen torturing myself because upstate New York wasn't glamorous enough for my sparkle, I had no idea. I've had to learn the hard way how cool ordinary life was: nice parents, good school, great friends on my softball team, fun gassing with the boys, and then *wham* – true love. Heavenly! Seth caused me a whole batch of chills and thrills from the get-go.

I was *sooo* foxy back when he came roaring up to my high school on his cruiser, even if I was only 4' 10". The year before, when I was sixteen, I'd had to get an e-pal from another country for English and my mum wouldn't let me hook up with a stranger, so she phoned around up to Nova Scotia where we had some shirttail cousins – my great-grandpa came over from Scotland – and one of them got me Seth's address.

Right away he sent photos for me to download and seeing him gave me little chills. He was not too tall and he looked strong, with blue eyes and a ruddy complexion, just the type to send me swooning. He looked straight into the camera and paid no attention to the pretty girls swamped around him. Just friends I guess. He also sent plenty of snaps taken during his motorcycle rides along these beautiful rocky shores surrounded by green forests. The scenes looked like some kind of fairyland to me since I'd been stuck growing up out in the sticks of rural Maine.

My senior year I fell deep into a dreamy romance river over Seth. The months passed with us on the phone and messaging each other every night, and then – there he was, right in my arms, and shortly into my knickers, as mum calls them. After I graduated we let my parents pull off a proper wedding with plenty of brew and napkins that said "Seth & Janie Forever." I waved goodbye to my US of A life and we rode north to Hali, or Halifax as it says on the maps, where I expected my days would each be like a sweet cherry in a shiny bowl.

We rented a crib in a converted two-story that had seen grander days. We had a bedroom upstairs and a sitting room with a kitchenette next to the washroom downstairs. Our bedroom looked out over the city toward the sea. Seth had a job in shipping calculating load weights and routes and rates. I fit into the city life pretty well and I even learned to say *eh*, like a question, as "Nice day, eh?"

When Seth's cousin from Galway came to visit we dubbed him "The Irish." He was taller than Seth and had the same complexion, but he seemed a little slack around the jaw. At first I liked him even though my Scots Grandma had taught me, "Never trust an Irishman." I even welcomed having him staying with us – sleeping on the couch with most of his gear stuffed behind the furniture. This worked until he started leaving his clothes and shoes and socks lying around everywhere. He also shed his red hair all over the washroom and bellowed these wake-the-dead snores we could hear echoing up the stairs.

I was working in a pet shop with crazy shifts and needed to sleep when

I could catch a few winks, so I asked Seth to tell him it was time for him to find his own place. Seth just gave me an, "EH-yuh," and said, "I think I'll tow that one alongside for a bit." Seth didn't make friends other than biker-buddies easily, so I played along.

Next, The Irish bought a big-ass Harley and I knew he'd gotten some kind of work visa and would be staying longer. Seth took to riding with The Irish every day after they got off work and on weekends with me stuck at Pet Parade working split shifts. I started to get the lonesomes, feeling really blue. Then I had worse news. Beer didn't count when it came to drinking in Hali and Seth never took more than a mickey of Scotch on his bike; only now The Irish had started bragging up his "fifth in the saddle."

One day at work this big mama smirked at me and said, "Hey Janie. I seen Seth's cuzzin' stiverin' drunk with his bike up the tarmac over at St. Mary's scarin' the girls. He's a good one to get nicked, eh?" I flushed red and turned my back – she had a ruddy nose and pudgy fingers like raw sausages, so I figured she hoisted a few at the pub herself. When I asked Seth about The Irish bothering girls, he had nothing at all to say and I couldn't face up to the cuz without a husband to back me. No fairyland for me, eh? Still, it all felt natural – before the wreck.

Finally I had a weekend off for a big ride on the cycles and we got away from Hali right after work Friday, Seth with me snuggled behind him and The Irish with a new hottie clinging to his backside. The roads were greasy with rain although the weather was set to clear up overnight. We zigzagged out of city traffic and onto a two-laner before dark, so we stopped for a break and a brew. After a couple of pints we started to load up and I saw The Irish had gotten staggerin' drunk.

"We better stay off the road," I said, "The Irish could get us all killed."

Seth shook his head and scowled at me! "Oh, don't be owly, Janie. Come on now."

"Wha's goin' on?" The Irish called out after he saw I wasn't getting on our bike.

"Janie's just a little spooky girl," Seth yelled. Then he smiled a little and patted my cheek, promised we'd stop soon – just marvel on up the road to a sweet lodge only sixty klicks away along a quiet, scenic stretch. I climbed on again and tightened my grip around his middle, leaning my head over next to his left shoulder so I could see the road ahead. We roared off out of the parking lot, and that was the last thing I remembered when I came to a couple of days later in the hospital.

I found myself trussed up in white sheets with visions of blurry faces looming in and out above me. My arms were strapped down, my brain felt fuzzy, and somehow I couldn't stop thinking about my hands. I couldn't free my arms even with pulling and tugging at the restraints so it was actually a few days before I knew what had happened. The whole time I could have sworn I was beating off boredom by moving my hands. I passed the hours spreading my palms, popping my double-joint thumbs, and then scrunching each hand into a fist – left, right, left, right, like a marching band.

Seth came and went, playing the good hubby, only he kept ducking his head, wiping his eyes, and blowing his nose. I was too groggy to wonder what was up. Little did I know a whole world of handicapped was soon to be mine, because there was nothing down at the ends of my arms. The bike engine had kept running for too long with my hands trapped under the exhaust pipe. Cooked.

You could say the whole wreck was Seth's fault. It was his idea to share digs with The Irish and I think he knew all along the cuz was no good for us. He couldn't admit it because it would have taken him a notch down from being a manly-man. The police told us The Irish was trying to pass Seth and me when he'd lost control. He and the fast girl flew right over a barrow pit and slammed into a rocky cutaway. Since they hadn't put their helmets on when we left the pub, it was a fat DOA cinch in a ditch. When I heard how they'd ended up, I just said, *Thank you, Thank you, God,* and if I sound soured-off, so be it. Saved me the trouble, eh?

My life in recovery began as soon as I got on my feet. I did well in the amputee rehab room even though I had many raw hours to put in. I was sweating it out one day when my specialist waltzed in with a big smile on his face and said he'd arranged for me to get prostheses in a *myoelectric* style. A company in Edinburgh called Touch Bionics had agreed to design a free promo-set just for me. Although they'd have long black, bony style fingers, I could design the palms and fingertips to look the way I wanted them to. What with the shock of the burning and all, I was in no mood for sugar-pie and I went a bit Goth. I even met with a tattoo designer and had him draw up some sketches for the decorated parts he assured me would look totally cunning.

"What's your main message with these new hands?" he asked.

103

"I want something a little for show, so's no one will sad-sack me, like, 'Oh honey, I'm so sorry you have to wear those ugly old things.'" We looked over several designs for the palms, and I picked a skull-shape done out with thistle flower cutaways. The artist wasn't done though.

"These studded wrist-bracelets I just got in would accent your prosthetics and they're only forty dollars," he offered. "I mostly sell them to biker girls."

I bought the bracelets to wrap over the straps hooking the prossies onto my stubs. My bubble burst when the hands came because the fingers looked like claws. After a good long cry, I managed to talk myself into learning how to use them. I spent a lot of time on bio-feedback pushing thoughts at them to where I could finally just think *open, grab, hold,* and *let go,* imagining each command as if my real hands were still there. I started using the stupid clunkers even though I was sorry I'd gotten curvy fake-fingernails that kept snagging everything.

I will say they were cool backscratchers. Seth and I got off on the whole I'm-coming-to-get-you thing. I'd "WOOOHOOO" and he'd yell, "No, Janie, No! Oh please don't, please …" and then I'd chase him up the stairs and we'd leap on the bed and boogie. We even got matching skeleton tats on our arms. Only I still had black times. One day it came to me how *if* I wanted to murder someone, the prossies would be great because I could choke the victim and the police could never track any fingerprints. Eh?

Unfortunately my bionics weren't good for holding a job. My manager back at the Pet Parade took one look at them and said he'd already hired someone else. So I tried cocktail waitressing at the Seahorse where Seth and his mates drank. Naturally I had to start on rush hour shifts and because my stupid prossies were bigger than my real hands I kept whacking things. I had to wear these slippery rubber gloves so customers wouldn't creep out, plus I kept spilling drinks to where the bartender called foul on me.

After I got fired and the romance of the Goth gave out, I started wishing maybe Seth's hands had been under the bike with mine. For better or for worse, you know?

So I went to the health clinic crying these big-ass tears and they bargained some trade-ins so I fit better into a pair of kid's models. The "Scampies" wouldn't work for cocktailing, although the smaller size meant I could at least work my phone better and maybe find another job. They were a two-finger-thumb combo with accordion-style padding on the fingers. They didn't snag my clothes so much, but they weren't any good for the rough and tumble playtimes Seth and I had gotten used to.

I started complaining to my tech at the clinic about the bulky finger padding and he added in a vibrator function which turned out to help Seth relax before we did stuff. He took some time getting used to the zgzgzgzg feeling before he came to like it. And where he used to be totally biker-on-the-road-for-life, he decided he wanted me to prove his sperm was hot by giving him a son (of course it would be a boy), one he could teach how to be a manly man. For me, prossies instead of hands just didn't fit with mothering an infant. When I said, "No baby!" Seth kind of blew up.

"You've been all sookie for nighin' onto months and months!" he yelled. "You're not sick, dammit. Get over it, Janie. I want us to be *normal!*"

Wasn't Seth a fine one to say *normal* I thought. "A mum needs hands to hold a baby, warm hands," I told him. He stewed about my refusal for a few weeks and then started badgering me to give in. I still wouldn't, so he tore down the curtains and slammed pots into the wall and kicked in the washroom door. When he cooled out, we looked at the mess and then we both cried. Afterward I didn't complain so much about his riding, riding, riding and spending hours and hours at the pub. Not much loving came my way though.

After I synced with the Scampies, I got a job at the city zoo. My babies there took right to my Scampies when I turned on the vibes. I was working in the snake-pit, as we called the Reptile House, and, contrary to what you might think, even creepy-crawlers can be very affectionate when given the soft touch. It's so cute the way they curl up and slither their tongues. The only standoff was a Black Mamba – always in a pithy mood, that one – and my boss forever sent me to calm him down since his neurotoxins wouldn't get to my real flesh. He tore up the soft poly covers on the Scampies' fingers and thumbs a few times. Luckily the zoo insurance paid for new ones. And I cached a few ounces of his venom to store in the freezer just in case I needed to protect myself sometime. Life goes on, you know.

My recovery made me awfully touchy about hands. I used to think hands had a sense of purpose and shaped themselves to their calling: butcher – knife, baker – dough, candlestick maker – maybe finger flames. Anyway, I started seeing long, skinny fingers as spiders and short ones as pudgies.

In cases of murder, Spiders would go for knives, pudgies for clubs, and knuckle-knockers would land a few deadly uppercuts. Now with poison, any old hands – or prossies – would do.

One winter's day when I was feeding the sluggy reptiles, a man I didn't know from Adam came in while I was handling one of the pythons. Right away I noticed this guy's long, smooth fingers with the knuckles modestly straight. Topside, his nails were buffed shiny and when he reached up to rub his chin I could see his thumbs were long too, so his grasp would be firm and comforting. If he ever made a movie featuring hands, he'd surely finger-stroll to an Oscar.

I wondered if he was a serpent addict because we didn't get many casual visitors to the snake pit in the winter. When the temperatures outside got really cold, we heated up the tropical snakes so they'd be more active and help us attract visitors. When the few tourists we attracted wandered in they helped the reptile division pay down the feed bills. Live rats could get expensive.

The visitor watched while I fed Billy, the python, and got him back in his cage, all snugged up to a heat lamp. I was wearing satin mittens because his dry skin meant he'd been losing a lot of scales. Then, when I slid the mitts off, there were my Scampies in full view. The visitor sucked his breath in with a whoosh as if he had a balloon to blow up and said, "I can't believe you were using those prosthetics. You must have practiced a lot."

My throat clammed shut and I couldn't think how to answer. Finally, I said, "No, I just whomped these on when they gave them to me and it's been upsy-daisy ever since."

Next he asked a lot of questions about how I lost my real hands and what the rehab was like. He took so long I had to tell him my manager would be whipping my tail off if I didn't get back to work. He wrote a number on the back of his card and gave it to me.

"I've never seen anyone manage those, uh, prosthetics so well, Miss. I'm a surgeon and I believe you are a candidate for transplants."

I said, "What, for me?" and then he said he wanted to be the head physician in charge of a double hand transplant, and I might be just the person he was looking for because of my "dexterity," which I took to mean my brain was still thumbs-up – even without real thumbs.

"Yeah, sure," I said. "These prossies were paid for by the Canadian Health Service and I don't think you'll find any real hands hanging out around the clinic."

"I'm from the Brigham and Women's Hospital in the states where we doctors sometimes get generous research funding for new procedures," he explained.

Well, I thought, maybe I wasn't done with the U S of A after all. Even though this Doc sounded pretty know-it-all, his swag gave me a little thump, thump somewhere south of my heart, the way I used to feel when Seth gave me the let's-do-it look. I truly missed Seth being my swooney lover man. I stuck the Doc's card in my pocket and all day I thought about calling him. The way he praised my use of the Scampies, the idea of having hands again, and the opportunity to help him be the top Doc on the morning news? It all sounded good. Maybe too good.

I started imagining how reporters would ask me stuff. Do you like having hands again? How does it feel to see them when you wake up in the morning? Do you think the hands will be worth all the time you'll spend learning to work them?

One day I was in a coffee shop watching a woman with her new baby. Suddenly I thought maybe with new hands we really could have a baby. Seth would get to teach his son manly things, and we'd might actually get back to our before-the-wreck selves. I even admitted to myself how the whole prossie gig had turned crappy even before Dr. Bob brought up the transplant idea.

I was tired of hiding the raw spots where the prossie straps chafed my arms bloody. My stubs hurt – sometimes shooting pains up my arms till my brain would shiver. And I couldn't stop thinking about my old hands. I'd even tried doing some *ohm* humming stuff to strangle off the phantom hands, but they held on. Some days I was like a big sack of boohoo blues. Finally one night I took a deep breath and asked Seth, "Hey, what if I could have hands again?"

"Hell, eh? Have you lost your mind?"

I filled him in on the surgeon's proposal for a double transplant and we knocked the idea back and forth for a while. Finally, he said yes, he'd go to Boston with me for the operation. He'd even heard about motorcycle groups he could approach. "I'll get in with the Red Emeralds and cruise stateside with the Yanks for however long it takes you, Janie." He held me in his arms a bit before heading out to the pub, and I bawled onto his shirt-shoulder because it was the nicest thing he'd offered to do for me in a long, long time.

The next day when I punched the Doc's number into my cell, I was so shaky I had to steady one Scampy with the other. Happily he answered right away and said to call him Dr. Bob. He sounded really excited and promised I'd get a full-service, all-expense paid operation and he'd hook me up with a clinic right there in Hali to do the paperwork.

"I'm in. Let's do it now during slow-time at the zoo," I said.

The clinic people promised to pass my Scampies on to a needy child after the op and Seth finagled a half-leave to where he could work a little out of the shipping company's Boston office. When the Brigham and Women people sent our plane tickets, we flew stateside so the Doc and his crew could get me ready for the big op. And to wait for a pair of hands to crop up.

When we got to the hospital it was like they'd rolled out a red carpet, although I hardly ever saw Dr. Bob. My days were soon filled what they called *teamwork*.

"Show me how your Scampies function," the nerve Doc said. Now you may remember the Scampies only came with a thumb and two fingers. I showed off how well I could use them by picking a comb out of my purse and fluffing my hair all pretty with the left, and then I opened and closed a safety pin with the right. "Outstanding!" he crowed. "You have the best nerve control we could ask for. Oh and, um nice meeting you, Janie."

The nurses weren't so busy. They eased out long descriptions of how the hands would be rushed to Brigham and Women's because they'd only be *viable* for a few hours after the *demise* of the donor. They hoped my operation would only take eighteen or so hours. "You'll be in Intensive Care for several days until things settle down," the head nurse explained.

Other specialists came and went, heart, lungs, liver – day after day – some with diagrams and lists, some with pictures. They went on about needles in my veins, stitching on the transplants, immunosuppressant meds – lots of other big words I couldn't follow – then the rehab. This is not to mention how I was poked and prodded and EKGed and X-rayed 'til I felt like a hoppy frog pinned down on a dissecting table. Toward the last, the whole op went blurry in my mind and I just *uh-huhed* in the pauses while the talkers droned on.

At least Seth was all charged up and positively glowy with bragging about me to his new friends in the cycle club. And I admit I was looking forward to being on camera after the operation. Me in a cool get-up holding my new hands up for everyone to see! If I'd paid more attention to the Doc's team, I might've settled down to the problem at hand before I gave the final go-ahead to Dr. Bob.

A pair of hands became available during our third week in Boston and I was rushed into pre-op. When the Doc came into my room the night before the operation, I made a couple of jokes with him so I could see his dimples, silly things like: Will I be able to play the piano when this is over? No? Well, I couldn't play it before so I hoped you could throw in a little *night music …*

Before the op got going, the meds gave me a *la la la* sleepy time and Seth whispered me into sweet dreams. He claimed he hugged my neck the whole time. I never should have let him stay with me and not just because of the bloody stump work. Later on he started saying how the surgery was trippy with thirty or forty people shifting around, going in and out. He asked me if I remembered how they'd shown me the new hands when Dr. Bob brought them out of their case. Seth had a good look and the ugly new hands gave him the willies.

So I asked him why not stop the whole works right then? He didn't have an answer, nothing at all. Maybe he wanted me to be the woman of his dreams like I was before the wreck – foxy and sweet at the same time. Or maybe he felt guilty about him and The Irish costing me my own hands. Now I'll be wearing someone else's hands till kingdom come. The new ones will never, ever match my old ones and I'll be totally attached to parts of someone else's otherwise dead body for the rest of my life.

After the wreck I'd adapted some to the prossies, only then I this took a stupid chance on new hands and now I'm stuck with these monkey paws stitched to my stubbies. Think about it, when you look down and see your own hands, what do you see? Freaks? No, you see familiars.

And you may have heard how some woman talks with her hands, or, how some man can't make a point without jabbing his finger at you. So, the hands I have now? They talk too much and they look awful. No one in my family would be caught dead wearing them. On bad days I imagine there must be some spirit hovering over its ugly skeleton and *ooh oohing* about not having any hands to wear on Judgment Day.

After the operation there were a few T.V. interviews with the cameras mostly on Dr. Bob. Didn't he look glowing! I was the problem. My face couldn't lie about how unhappy I was with the newbies, and no twinkly stars lit up my eyes. Someone offered me a book deal and then I never got the contract. A movie producer called and he's supposedly still looking for a backer. So now when I wear the newbies to bed (because I have to) they start itching to get even with my soon-to-be ex.

It seems like a lifetime ago when I rode into Hali on the back of a Moto-Guzzi thinking my new daily life would be heavenly and being a Nova Scotian would be a stroll on the beach with lobster din-dins once a week. I looked for Seth to be at my side by day and in my arms on moonlit nights. Now I'm back in rehab, he's moved out and asked his Boston boss for a transfer to Australia because he has these nightmares where my hands choke his neck or gouge his eyes out.

If I could really take these spoilers off and leave them on the kitchen counter at night, he might be here today. I pretend I can, hiding them under my pillow, hoping they won't start whispering little twinges about slipping an ounce or two of Black Mamba juice in his coffee the next time I see him. If I see him. And if we do meet up to sign the divorce papers, I'm not so sure these raggedy paws will even scribble out any *Mrs. Seth So and So* signature.

On the other hand, maybe this won't be my last act after all. Maybe I'll rip on through the curtains of my poor-me routine and star in a brand new US of A extravaganza. Dr. Bob asked me to shoot him a text if I ever wanted to do a follow up session on the *Today Show* with him and the parents of my new hands. I started realizing I might just be freaky enough to go viral. I could get myself a blog, and maybe land a role on one of those reality TV shows. I might even find a handsome new manly man who'd *normal* me right back into a New York state of mind. Eh?

Hannah-Marie Nelson
University of Minnesota-Twin Cities

Here

Samantha watered our maple tree every day. The tree was over ten times her age and height, but she watered it as meticulously as the potted marigolds, petunias, and peonies. Repeatedly I'd explained to her that only the feeble flowers needed an afternoon drink, but she faithfully repri-manded my callousness towards the tree's hydration needs. She always disregarded my instructions, spritely circling the bulbous base of a trunk she couldn't wrap her arms around with a sporadic stream of sustenance, humming the maple a midday lullaby with the grace of a dying child. Her middle name, Hannah, meant the grace of God in Hebrew.

Sam taught me that even angels need watering cans on Earth. Hers was pink with cartoon flowers speckled across the plastic. Five flowers fabri-cated from five puffy petals and a circle. Her watering can became mine though, repossessed by order of death. On the handle where her helping hands used to hold, my aging hands gripped, indirectly holding hers once more when I watered the marigolds by her headstone. Marigolds were my daughter's favorite flower.

When I arrived in Chicago at my sister's house, I had wet petals plastered against the soles of my high heels. Not marigold petals but unwelcome hitchhikers that had caught a ride; I scraped the soiled trespassers onto the sidewalk. The foreignness of the petals coerced me into bitterly recollecting the foreignness of my new, northern home. My indulgent Dixie house with the maple tree had been lost to the federal force of foreclosure, taken away by taxes I, a kindergarten teacher, couldn't pay when my parents too "passed away."

I loathe that expression because death doesn't casually pass by like some sauntering summer cloud. The Reaper doesn't tip-toe past guised in camouflaging quiet; he crashes in with a cacophony of immutable morbidity. Corpses may lie unperturbed and forgotten, but active death loathes being so blatantly ignored. Death is boisterous and chaotic and deafening and uproarious all in one moment's passing because time can pass away when ailing people cannot.

My time spent in Chicago with Opal, my older sister, and her husband, Tom, kept on passing away until I was relocated to my current home. I get quite lonely here; here being I don't know exactly where. Supposedly I wound up wherever here is because I "lost my marbles." I find this predicament to be an awful shame because I'm sure I didn't lose all my marbles at once; maybe I'm crazy, but I'm not careless. One by one my precious little marbles must've been rolling away right out of some damning hole in my head, leaving a glass trail all the way back to Alabama where I'm sure a few fell. I wish I would've felt them falling.

I miss Opal here, but I don't miss her house. In my opinion, it was a stretch to call that tiny, two-room set up a house anyhow. There wasn't even a door to divide the rooms, just a bolt of ragged cloth the couple fancied to call a curtain. Plus, the place really only encompassed half a house because the top rooms belonged to different tenants. That south side dump cowered beside Opal and my lost childhood home, the one with the maple tree and clean sheets.

I set up residence in a motel for a couple months before I came to Chicago because I didn't want to be the washed up Southern belle freeloading off of her baby sister, but when I lost my job at the elementary school, my money stream ran dry. I used to be rich. The kind of rich without boundaries or budgets or bankruptcy. The kind that comes from family fortunes. My parents couldn't hide our financial duress from me once they died though. The loss of my lavish lifestyle and even my meager teaching salary shot my pride in the back of the head. A kill shot.

The motel I resided at was called The Black Panther, a seedy spot down a rutted road on the bad side of Birmingham. I stayed in room 209, and there weren't clean sheets there either. Many of my marbles must still be strewn across that room, under the god-awful floral covers of my squeaky, single bed in the cracked, blue, faux-leather couch cushions, rolling around the plug of the yellowed bathtub's drain.

I'm sure one slipped away the day I brought Tessa inside those wood-paneled walls. Tessa was one of my students, only five years old, and I'll be damned if she wasn't the spitting image of my sweet Samantha. They were miles apart personality wise, sassy and skeptical Tessa versus my trusting and kind-hearted Sam, but whenever Tessa kept her back-talking mouth closed, I could too-easily pretend she was my Samantha. Tessa tirelessly taunted my memory's ability to remember, to recall anything at all. She'd have her head tilted one way into the light, or I'd see her from behind and she *was* Samantha. Too often she was Samantha. Too often I played the fool. I missed my daughter with such ferocity that one Monday after a weekend of mourning among the marigolds, I suppose I forgot that Tessa was not actually my Sam. I took Tessa home with me, and that's how I lost my teaching position.

Tessa wasn't the last Sam imposter though. I found another when Opal gave birth to a healthy baby girl while I was staying in Chicago. For months I watched that glorious baby morph into my Samantha as she grew. The resemblance was uncanny even at her young age, and this time I didn't fight my forgetfulness; I embraced it like a long lost child, like *my* long lost child. I craved disillusionment, so I let Sam be reincarnated in a different vessel, finally unleashing my repressed hunger for motherhood. That beautiful baby was my second chance. When I was home alone with her, I'd rock her possessively in my arms and coo soothingly to her that her real momma was here now, stroking Sam's chestnut hair, singing her real name, Samantha, over and over into her uncomprehending ears while marbles shattered on the floor. Tom came home early from work one day though and heard me, and that's how I wound up here.

"I don't like to shave my knees, so I do so sparingly. Yes, in all seriousness, your best bet on where to uncover indecently overgrown stubble squatting savage-like atop my legs is indeed my knees. Your mapping fingers might instinctively flinch back at the uncharted, pokey patches, as they bravely scout out the peaks of the caps or behind the bony bumps, but know that neither I nor my knees offer any condolences. Now that I'm knee deep in this unladylike predicament though, I might as well reveal that on the sides of my ankles, on and around the bulbous bones, your thorough fingers are also likely to find some stray strands standing at attention, ready to prick your pin cushion fingertips. What finagling strands, the villainous lot of them foiling the valiant razor's edge more often than not, yet, this isn't the hair's victory to claim, it's the bones. It's always the bones.

The bones, the knights of shining marrow, the cliché, heroic obstacles that gallantly rescue the stubble from decapitation; hairy damsels in distress whisked away from the guillotine. Bound in a sausage casing of flesh that is too easily severed and drowning in blood that too easily jets forth from their thin wrappers, the bones of my knees and ankles jut out from my meat like a rocky overhang, jeopardizing the razor's smooth ascendancy of my leg's mountains of skin, mountains of cellulite. Such hazardous handholds are meant to be avoided, and my razor takes a side detour around these danger zones. It's a logical approach to cliff scaling but not a logical approach to the code of womanhood.

Soggy soap and razor blades canoodling in shower cubbies. Surely, that's a fun factoid for the textbooks. Oh yes, the dear sweet textbooks, the ones that will detail the code of womanhood my generation adhered to closer than a clean shave between blades and bristly hair made coarse by such religious removal. Generations of students to come will glance back over time's detached blockade, snickering as snootily as only ignorant present dwellers can before the characterizing whispers that encase bizarre tidbits of bygone times begin."

My little sister Julia wrote that. She was my other sister, the forgotten sister. I found the preceding excerpt in her therapy journal after she killed herself in May. Julia had to die though. Julia was crazy. For all her hateful talk of detached textbooks wrongly dissecting the morsels of her time, Julia would've read the pages of *her* history until the inked words smudged away, her bony hands flipping back and forth through *her* chapter until the educatory picture of an old-fashioned razor faded from her finger's aggressively loving touches. Faded and smudged away like a teenage life in turmoil when all Julia wanted was to be remembered, immortalized, perpetuated. She wrote ill of a disdained practice of her life, but she'd ravish the feast of the future generation's discombobulation. Julia wanted to be an enigma, a conundrum, a mystery.

I don't know who she was directing this particular rant at. Maybe it was womankind or society as a whole, but whatever audience she would have rendered, rapt by her defiance, would've remained blissfully unaware of their writer's ending. Keep in mind endings aren't usually happy for depressed anorexics with hairy knees and ankles though. April showers are supposed to bring May flowers, but only showers of carmine came, and with them I brought May flowers, white lilies, to Julia's gravestone where she's immortalized in granite. Silly Julia, the code of womanhood never said to shave your wrists. Too bad the bones there couldn't stop her.

Yes, Opal was my sister and Julia was my sister too, but I don't miss Julia as much. Opal was normal. I idolized her normalcy. Julia was crazy; the kind of crazy that whittled a fifteen-year-old into an abstract bone sculpture hardly held up by the jagged spine she used as a tent pole for her hanging skin. Her jagged edges were hard to look at when I could still remember her days of soft, sloping sides. Julia thought sloping sides were sloppy though and that her harsh edges enhanced her living artistry. Her bones were the only part of her body she didn't try and conceal.

For years she hid her nails with black nail polish because underneath they were cracked from malnourishment. In fact, we buried her with that fittingly morbid black still staining the fingertips she had drenched in red. She had always looked quite fetching in red.

I'm not allowed nail polish in here. The liberty to douse my nails with

114

unnatural hues is a freedom I never thought I'd come to miss, but now I'm here wrought with longing. Who knew I'd ever be jealous of Julia? My envy hardly holds though when I know her fingers have rotted away by now. She's finally rotted down to just bones, her dream come true.

***

"What color would you like?" mother asked, gesturing to the patio table where the dozen or so nail polish bottles stood.

"Hm," I mused, hovering a smooth hand over each one, "I want the red one! The red one, mommy!" I exclaimed, bouncing on my chair cushion. When mother went to grab the bottle I was vigorously gesturing to, she accidentally bumped it with her rumpled hand, the glass bottom grating against the metal tabletop before it began to freefall. Red on the bricks.

***

Mother swatted my hand. "Stop picking at your nail polish!" she admonished in a whisper fitting of church. My thumbnail was methodically chipping away at the other fingers' carmine coatings when my hands were supposed to be reverently clasped. I hung my head as if in prayer, but I was admiring the shining flecks as they fell into the lap of my mint green dress, gathering in a treasure pile in the valley of drooping fabric between my legs.

I momentarily lifted my eyes to mumble, "Sorry," and promptly returned to picking away. I concluded that mother must've spread the paint layers on thicker on my left hand because those fingertips' coatings came off easier. On my right hand, however, misshapen chunks remained stuck to the middle of my nails like dark icebergs that I couldn't melt away.

***

Maybe I don't miss the nail polish after all. Yes, I think I might only miss picking it away. I've always had that picking urge, that vexing sensation that pricks at my knuckles and pools restlessly in the joints of my fingers when they are idle. This used to worry me as a child because mother always told me that idle hands are the devil's playthings, but her proverb doesn't plague me now that I've already confirmed its accuracy.

I've fallen back into my childhood picking habits here because my hands have nothing to preoccupy themselves with. Yes, here their schedule is as blank as the walls. They have infinite time to crawl across the barrier of my body between them and meet in awkward, sharp entanglements.

They pick and peel away the calloused skin surrounding my nail beds that has coarsened from being peeled away so many times before. They pick at their fellow nails too and rip off the meager pieces still left to be harvested. They do this until there is nothing left but the red.

The silence is unsettling here. The room's resounding quiet creeps into my ear drums, nesting far from the reach of the fingertips I plunge in after it. The softer the room's silence, the louder the noiselessness grows, soaking up every secret sound and amplifying it ruthlessly within my head until the quiet vibrates between my scalp and skull. Soon the sound of my breath is a roaring storm beating about my white-walled cage, and only I can save myself from the cyclone manifesting inside my mind. The hurricane of each inhale and exhale is maddening, deafening, excruciating. To rescue myself from the tempest drawing power from my lungs, I stop breathing. I cease to fuel the wind whipping around me, but I can't halt the thundering thumps of my heart deep in my chest even as I try to claw my way to the source. I can't scrape through my skin and dig my way down without the nails I've picked away though, so I must surrender to the silence.

Even I find the irony in my newfound relationship with sound, however, because all throughout my childhood I prayed for silence, for peace within the walls where I used to dwell. The walls there weren't white; they were pink. A pale, peaceful pink that never seemed to match the chaotic sounds that ricocheted between them. They threw the noises of yelling and bawling and battling back and forth across the gaping space where I laid feebly in my bed. As the war song of the fighting of my parents leaked under the bottom of my door, I took cover beneath the bedsheets, curled up on my side, watching the solitary candle I'd light like a sign of surrender when the quarrels began.

I found a numbing distraction watching the candle's wick wither away as the dauntless flame clambered higher, pushing the wax ever lower. Yes, there was a certain serenity that ascended as the melted wax dribbled down. Every hot, diving drop was a tear the candle shed instead of me. I'd chosen a fresh candle for that special night of anarchy because I'd felt I'd need an unfatigued flame's sway working against the disorder inside of me. As the fight inflated though, I knew this was a new kind of argument, a kind that couldn't be eased in my mind by the new flame of an old distraction. This strange duel had a new subject of debate. The usual sparring topics of money and my sisters and I had been passed over for the matter of infidelity. Never before had my father accused my mother of being unfaithful and never before had his temper escalated so far out of hand. Yes, he must've lost control of his hand because their duel of words turned to a fight of few words and many slaps and sobs.

My mind was in frenzy as my unblinking eyes locked in on the sole flame. Distraction was replaced by action. I too lost control of my hand as it floated out to grasp the cold candlestick holder, and I lost control of my feet as they swung out of the blanket and across the floor. My head assured me I only wanted to watch the flame's reflection in the dark window as I moved, but my hand wouldn't raise it towards the window sill. My detached eyes merely watched as the light crossed the glass night sky with no more power than they had watching a shooting star. The flame was just a star, a harmless star that my hand offered as a gift to the pink curtain folds. My innocent star was consumed by the cloth though, and I feared it had fizzled out, eaten alive by the drapes gaping, pink lips, but then it reappeared in a blaze of brilliance. The delicate twinkle carved through the curtain, gracefully sacrificing the fabric of the universe for which now it was the sun. Here, surveying the solar flares that engulfed the celestial sphere, I was finally hypnotized. No longer did I hear the sharp echoes of beaten skin or scared cries for mercy. I too was consumed, sacrificed, engulfed. I left my masterpiece, my heaven, only when my sisters dragged me out.

Javeria Kausar
Maris Stella College (India)

Still Alive

My breathing's fast. It's the first time that I am in such a situation.

His breathing seems normal; it's as though he has been doing this all his life.

I hide behind a crumbling wall, peering through its cracks; for the state I am in, I have to be vigilant.

He stands a small distance away from me, a too-big rifle across his back. With a small gun in one hand and a big cigarette in the other, he kicks rocks on the cracked ground to make way. There are several people around him, none living. And all their eyes seem to be fixed upon this rugged smoker, with unwavering accusation.

He does not seem to care. If anything, he looks as if it is the most natural scene in the world: crumbling houses, dying people, and a desert painted red; howling young, weeping old, and a long-lasting, eerie silence and numerous lifeless gazes. It's the environment he's been used to. It has not been long since he first saw such sights.

He starts kicking every body on the ground as if killing them was not enough.

A body twitches as he digs his spiked shoes into its face. I hear a gunshot. I instinctively scream and shut both eyes and ears as though that would keep reality out.

The next time I use my ears, I hear footsteps. The kind of sound that is produced when someone too small wears heavy boots not made for him. I peer through holes in the wall again. I see him approaching slowly. He walks a bit awkwardly in baggy pants. They too, do not seem to be meant for him.

Yet, he doesn't stumble. He seems sure of his footing. And he's coming right here where I cravenly wait for him.

He comes closer and easily smashes the withering wall with the back of that too-big rifle. I draw back. Not in fear, but in total disgust and regret at his present state. He ought to be somewhere else- someplace better.

118

After the dust settles, I see him more clearly. He rubs his eyes with his wrists violently, dangerously. He probably doesn't know how easily a gun's trigger can be pulled.

His eyes, finally clear, meet mine and a chill runs up my spine. Those bloodshot doe-eyes, sinking under heavy bags are enough to paint a miniature picture of his life.

There are no wrinkles of age on his face; only those of past confusion, disaster, and fear. He is only a scar of his past.

His lips are cracked, just like his life. His smile is nowhere in sight. Just like his future.

He lifts his rifle and takes aim. He closes one eye and focuses on different parts of my body as though looking for the right place to finish his work. He's dull, lifeless, and quite ready for his usual routine.

Suddenly, he lowers his gun and he stares. With those big deprived eyes, shedding invisible scarlet tears, he stares with those sunken, haunting eyes.

I look all around me. No one around. But I see something else. Something that is flashing in his previously lifeless eyes. A transient glint. A sudden unexpected return of a long-lost spark.

I feel encouraged. I swallow the lump of hopelessness and helplessness and stand up. His eyes are fixed on me. He doesn't move, still staring at me. He is gaping now. His fine jaw has dropped and he is visibly awed.

I want to go near him, but don't have the courage. Surprisingly, he drops his rifle and walks towards me in big flailing boots. For the first time, he seems to stumble, almost like a normal person. Somehow, he makes it to me.

He isn't looking at my face. I know because he would have to lift his head up. I'm not at all taller than average.

His head is bent and he seems to be staring at the little bag around my waist. He slowly raises his hand and brings it closer to me. I flinch but stay still with my eyes closed.

I can hear a soft sob and a sniff. I open my eyes to see that he had taken the tattered teddy-bear from my bag. I had found it several days ago under some old house's rubble. It seemed to have been there since a long time.

It was dirty and pathetic.

He hugs it and whispers in his native tongue. His tired eyes stream tears, washing his face. The fallen cigarette and guns say more than he could ever explain. His real self is out, brought by the tattered toy he used to play with not six months ago.

I look at him once again. Short and slender, wearing somebody else's clothes and doing somebody else's bidding without knowing why. A soldier of sorts.

Not even a teen yet.

Terrorized and traumatized, he's now terrifying others. His lost past, his lost innocence, and thoughts that he'd lost everything, his teddy's still here. He's still here.

Suppressed by war which sees no age, still his real self is alive.

Luke Valmadrid
University of Wisconsin-Madison

Vestige

She sighed. A sigh that stayed in the room because the wind never reached her. The old three-setting fan that her parents let her have from home was more noisy than refreshing, but on those 100-degree days, the small relief that it provided from the Louisiana heat felt worth it.

The trolley rolled noisily outside, and she wondered like she always did about why the city spent so much time and money on restoring a mode of transportation as inefficient as the trolley line instead of creating a bus system. Some people were willing to die for culture. People like her roommates. But like the city, she would turn a blind eye to her roommates' superficialities if they would just clean up after themselves.

Though at this point, she was numb to the heat, the noise, and her roommates' lack of etiquette, even more so because she had a decision to make. The kitchen looked small. Maybe if she knew some people who lived in that neighborhood…

"May!" She turned her head. "What's up, Ellen?"

"Are you coming with us tonight?" That's the girl she was before, but not anymore. "I can't, this chemistry problem set is –"

"Aww, you never want to hang out with us anymore." She didn't.

"No, I do, it's just that I've been putting this off all week, and also –" Her roommate was already out the door, waving her hand dismissively.

"Yeah, yeah, Ms. Academic, praise be."

May turned back to her desk and the lease on top of it.

It wasn't anything grandiose; she loved that word. It was just a normal studio apartment, acceptably clean and accompanied by a rent that felt doably-counterbalanced by waitressing and that small scholarship she received because of her dad's sharp salute. Other people would've passed on the apartment because of its distance from campus, but she saw a blank canvas. A vessel she could fill completely with her personality. Other people might've seen how torn the wallpaper was near the ceiling and the smell of antiquity, but in their place she strung Christmas lights and inhaled the scent of freshly baked pepper-bread. She would finally be able to make a place her own.

And then she shuddered. Because she remembered that she used to live alone, and why she just about begged these shallow witches to let her sublet from them. And –

She held her shoulders reflexively. Her skin froze, yet started to sweat, as if dreading the possibility of heat. Her breathing came in waves that became shallower and shallower. Her muscles tightened, pulling her limbs closer to her core. Her hands suddenly gripped her shoulders so tightly that they would leave dark imprints as ominous proof. Her forehead pressed into her knees, so that her tears fell quickly down between her legs. Anything to hide. Anything to make herself smaller. Because if she was smaller, then maybe he couldn't.

But he did.

He always did.

Then came the screams. She'd been getting better at muting them by firmly clasping her mouth onto the skin just above her knee, but that effort was solely for the comfort of others. To her, her screams were always deafening. Despite constantly assuring herself that she was fine (as others assured her then), it was a long time before she loosened.

And then came the feeling of absolute disgust, a loathing that unfairly couldn't find anyone else to hate but herself. Suddenly her hands weren't hers, her legs weren't hers, mouth – skin – she ran to the shower. Shivering in the heat, she mercilessly scrubbed herself red. Her breathing still erratic, she slowly raised her head and let the water run over her. She stayed like this a while.

Walking back into her room, she glanced at the clock: only an hour this time. Better. Always better, but never good.

She sighed. A sigh that stayed in the room because the wind never reached her, because if it did, it would pick her up because she was empty and send her into the sky. She thought that that might not be so bad.

The trolley rolled noisily outside, and she wondered like she always did about how no one heard her. Some people were willing to feign ignorance to keep peace of mind. People like her roommates. None of them had reached out to her, so easily falling into the habit of uniting by pointing

122

out "the strange." She heard them downstairs.

"What's she doing in there?"

"Chemistry problem set, my ass."

But at this point, she was numb to the heat, the noise, and her roommates' lack of humanity, even more so because she didn't feel like this decision was hers to make.

She signed her name on the lease.

Then she ripped it into shreds, allowing the fan to spin the stale air in a way that lifted the jagged pieces aloft, so that they almost believed that they were flying.

Callie Ann Marsalisi
Northeastern University

On Your Left

It was raining and she had just walked into a trash can. Not because of her own foolishness – she was looking where she was going, her phone safe and dry in her pocket – but because of someone else's.

A cyclist on the sidewalk! Unbelievable. Reckless. And now her right half was soaked in the front. She cupped her hand and tried to scoop away some of the larger drops that gathered on her skirt. Skirt, not raincoat, no, she hadn't known it was going to rain today. It was a rare day in March where you could get away with a skirt and tights and no coat over your sweater. Of course it rained.

She was only twenty minutes from home. She could be late to her interview or wet at her interview. She rocked back and forth on her heels. She could explain being wet better than being late.

But if she went home, she could go over her notes one more time. This was the sixth graduate school that she was interviewing for and they all seemed to get muddled up in her mind. Programs and scholarships and buildings that were all named similarly but not the same, details she didn't care about, interviewers' names that kept slipping her mind. None of it interested her anymore, so she had to work harder to remember. Reviewing her notes one last time would be good.

But she could explain being wet better than she could explain being late. She sighed and looked in her bag. When she had jumped out of the way of the cyclist, her bag had swung wildly away from her shoulder, and there was a chance her water bottle had spilled. If her water bottle had spilled, she would definitely have to go back home. She could get away with being wet, but her resume could not.

The lid of her water bottle was on tight and the inside of her bag was dry. She frowned into it the way she had frowned into the orange pumpkin pail the year her brother ate all of her Halloween candy. She had taken photos of the empty bucket, made copies, and taped them up all around the house. Like many of her "stunts," as her dad called them, this plan had worked.

Before he went out and bought her a bag of Skittles, her brother had spent a week embarrassedly tearing down pictures. Her uncle had found a well-hidden photo at Christmastime.

She shooed the memory away like a mosquito and forged on in the direction of the building where she was scheduled to meet the interviewer. This campus was close to home, which could save her money on housing and transportation. Her therapist had told her to look for "the small goodness" in every situation.

The sidewalk was nearly empty, so she hovered over to the left side, hugging the edges of buildings for what little cover they could provide. The rain did not seem to be letting up, but every once in a while the wind would turn it away from her. Her right side was about wet as it could get, so there wasn't much point in worrying about the rain, probably. That didn't necessarily make it better.

She walked by an old brick building, one that looked like it had once been a place to repair cars or sell car parts or something with cars – it had two enormous garage doors, and what else would you use those for? She looked at the closed and locked doors and wondered if she should have bought that old Civic from that guy two years ago. It wouldn't have set her back that much; maybe it would have helped her find a job and bring in some extra money.

But no, she was going to jet off across the country in search of the best graduate schools and she didn't want to have to buy and sell a car in such a short period of time. And the Civic hadn't looked very safe.

The building sat there, square and ugly, oblivious to her thoughts. She was glad it was closed. She was glad she didn't have to see mechanics running around, looking for parts and wiping their hands on their jeans. She was glad she didn't have to see any broken-up cars, waiting to see if they could be salvaged.

She reached the end of the brick building, fingers trailing on the corner, not wanting to let go. She turned and cupped the edge of the building in both hands as though she were going to shove it off its foundation. If another dumb cyclist decided to take up the whole sidewalk, maybe she'd find the strength to do just that. But right now, with the bricks and the rain and the empty sidewalk, she needed all of her strength just to keep walking. She pushed off the building like it was the center of the Earth and pivoted towards her destination.

Jennifer, she thought to herself. That was the name of the woman who was going to interview her. But it was spelled funny like Gennifer or Jennyfer. She had no idea what the woman's last name was or if she was a doctor or a professor or Her Majesty. All of that probably mattered more than how she spelled Jynnifer. But it was all coming up blank.

Her feet were soaked through, and she was glad she was wearing tights instead of socks. At least she wasn't stuck with feet that were soggy and heavy. Just soggy. She tipped her head back and drank some of the rain. This storm was relentless. Maybe drinking its water would help her out. Her wet hair rubbed against her back.

Just before the campus, she reached a crosswalk. The white lines were faded in the middle where students and professors and overeager moms on tour crossed back and forth every day. Her toe peeped into the intersection when tires shrieked behind her. She gasped and flailed for balance as a dark car – with the headlights out, because why not? – whipped around the corner, slammed into a left turn without stopping, and nearly went up on the far sidewalk.

She watched the car speed away, her wet hair sticking to her face, bag slipping down into the crook of her elbow. For a second, memories and rain washed over her. She did not get the license plate.

"Hey!" she yelled, long after the car was out of sight. "Hey! Watch where you're going! Fucking watch where you're going! You could hurt someone, you could put someone in a coma! You could put him in a coma!" She stood on the corner, shaking, watching the place in the road where the car had been. Slowly she moved just her eyes, sweeping them over the edge of the campus that had only recently come into view. Then she looked back after the car again. As she looked back and forth, slowly the rain started to ease.

She wondered if it was the same car from two months ago, but knew deep down that couldn't be the case. That car had been wrecked, totaled. She remembered looking at the bumper, wondering how it could still be held on by that two-inch strip of metal. She had stared at that bumper, burned it into her memory. But she hadn't gotten the license plate then, either. One of the cops had written it down.

Two months ago, she got the first callback from one of the eight graduate schools she applied to. It was her second choice, but she had turned them down. I can't leave my family right now, was all she had said. The man on the phone had hung up on her, after telling her to have a pleasant day. The second school called nine days later when things had stabilized, her parents sometimes both at home and not at the hospital. She had to turn down the second school too because she knew they couldn't afford it now. She had told her parents that her first choice never called. She would have turned down every other school, up until this one today, but her mom had insisted that she "move forward, keep moving forward."

She looked both ways and moved forward into the intersection. She crossed the street and climbed the hill towards the campus, keeping the clock tower on her right like Gynnifer had told her to. She reached the top of the hill, turned left, went down some stairs, passed the library, went up some other stairs, and finally found the building where her interview was scheduled to take place. She squished up the stairs, pushed open the heavy glass door, and took the first left.

There she found the ladies' room. It was a single room with a locking door and a hand dryer. She clicked the lock with her thumb, took off her shoes, and held them under the dryer. She held them up close by the opening, switching them in and out when her hands got too hot. The rest of her dripped onto the tile floor.

When her shoes were adequately dry, she slipped them on, checked her hair in the mirror, and left the bathroom. From there she turned back down the hallway, pulled open the door, crossed campus, tiptoed through the intersection, and headed back home.

Thaddeus Lenk
University of Michigan

An Evening Meal

The tavern sat at the edge of the desert. It was surrounded by arid land; rocky, and ill-suited for farming. In the distance, the roaming hills, the endless wastes of the desert could be seen. The tavern was a squat, two story building with a pub below and scant rooms above. It was wooden, its walls and doors worn down by sand and wind. Its stairs creaked and all together it was an abysmal establishment. A corral stood off to the side, a shelter for the weary horses of road worn travelers. The tavern was the only stop between the territory of the Bolides and that of the Tektites. It was the only hospitable place, situated in the worst stretch of inhospitable land possible. The tavern needed no name to distinguish itself for it was known far and wide simply as what it was; a brief respite from the burning heat of the sun, the harsh cold of the night, the pain of the whipping sand, and the dangers of the desert's hidden monsters.

It was also rumored to hold the most distinguished chef within the known kingdoms. The chef, an eccentric and an exile, had served under both the Feral King of the Bolides and the Everlasting Princess of the Tektites. His food and drink was renowned, and to many of the nobility and royal chefs of the region, traveling to his tavern was a rite of passage. However, the chef cared not for these ranks of nobility and honor. He treated each of his patrons equally, whether they were of marble halls and gilded rooms or denizens of the earth and soil, fingernails broken and hands covered in dirt. All were welcome to enjoy the confines of the tavern and the splendor of the chef's delectable madness.

Alwin rode, his body tired and mind exhausted, across the dry land separating the Bolides and Tektites. He rode with his brother, Costace, and their friend, Petra. The three were messengers; a lowly class abused by the nobility and merchants as tools to communicate. Evening was setting upon them and the waning light of the sun cut across the dry landscape. Alwin could hear the rancid cries of vultures overhead. In the distance, atop the crest of a hill, he spied the outline of the tavern. After a tiring day's ride, they would finally be able to rest.

The three messengers urged their mounts on, enticed by the thought of warm food and stiff drink. Their clothing was travel dirty, soiled by the elements and sickly sweat. Their horses, catching on to the excitement of their riders, urged themselves forward ever faster. They could not possibly

128

know it, but fresh water, oats, and a comforting roof overhead awaited them.

They came upon the tavern after a last, desperate gallop. In a haze of excitement, Alwin and the others left their horses in the hands of one of the tavern's porters and eagerly walked up to the front steps. This would be the first time any of them had visited the tavern and each was interested to see if reality would live up to the legend.

The door to the tavern creaked open on rusted hinges. Inside, Alwin was greeted by the warm glow of the pub. Several tables were scattered across the room, some filled and others barren. An imposing bar stood against one wall. It was lined with road-worn travelers and gilded nobility alike. An impressive stock of liquors sat gleaming behind the bar, the light dancing off their colorful bottles and deep, rich-looking liquor. Alwin and the others walked over to a table and sat down, letting out a sigh of relief. Their muscles unwound and their weary, sore limbs sank into the wood.

"Finally." He breathed out, looking from Costace to Petra.

Petra flashed Alwin a smile and brushed a strand of hair behind her ear. "I've got a feeling tomorrow's going to be worse."

Costace grunted in reply, too tired to speak.

An attendant adorned in road leathers, his face and body speaking from a lifetime of wandering the ruthless wastes of the known world, stepped to the table. His voice was gruff and to the point.

"There's two options. What'll it be?" He asked, handing a single, torn and worn scrap of paper to the scratched surface of the table.

Alwin and the others glanced at the paper. There were, indeed, two options. One promised a bounty of ribs, soaked in a delicate sauce, plenty of warm cornbread, and a choice drink from the bar. The second option was simple. It promised two small, measly ribs, a dry rub smeared on the meat the day before. There was no mention of accompaniment, and a simple tagline of *beer* sat next to the description of the ribs. Both options were a measly ten coppers.

Costace and Petra looked up at the attendant after no more than a glance at the scrap of paper.

"Number One Please!" They said in unison. Weary from the road and excited at their prospects, their eyes eagerly clung to the promises of the first option.

Alwin, though, stared at the scrap of paper for another moment. He felt the attendant's stare shift to him, exhausted anger radiating from his eyes. Alwin looked up slowly from the paper. He shifted his gaze from the attendant to the other patrons of the tavern. All around, he spied plates filled with mouth-watering ribs, piles of fresh, soft cornbread, and all manner of drink. Alwin's eyes turned back to the attendant.

"I think I'll have the number two, please."

The attendant sneered at Alwin. "It's not special."

"Excuse me?" Alwin asked.

The attendant ignored Alwin. He picked up the menu.

"The second meal isn't special. No one orders it, because it's a joke. The chef put it on there years ago as a prank. I've never had anyone order it. Don't think you're special."

Alwin stared at the attendant for a moment, thinking about his words. Alwin replied with a shrug.

The attendant gave a grunt and turned to go. Costace and Petra looked at Alwin, incredulous.

"What're you doing you idiot?" Petra asked.

"Seriously, brother. Since when did you grow so monkish?" Costace chided.

Alwin shrugged as the two dug into him. He wasn't quite sure himself. There had just been something, some quiet dignity about the whole ordeal that had enticed him. Even now, he questioned his choice. And his sanity.

After the questioning, the three fell into a quiet calm of conversation and laughter as they waited. Soon enough, the food arrived, bringing a pleasant smile to each of their faces. For Costace and Petra, heaping plates of moist ribs, succulent cornbread, and tall drinks of expensive liquor sat in front of them. For Alwin, a plate of two ribs, slightly dry, and a mug of thin, pale beer sat in front of him. As the other two dug in with vigor, Alwin looked at his plate for a moment. The attendant sneered at him when he'd handed over the food.

With an intrigued hand, Alwin reached out for the beer. He took a sip. It tasted more of water than beer. Setting down the mug, Alwin turned to his plate. He picked up one of the ribs and noticed the scant meat holding onto the bone. Alwin bit in and tasted the dry rub and the tender meat. Despite its size, the rib was enjoyable. The meat was well taken care of, the spices in the rub exciting and savory. However, it was by no means a spectacular meal; definitely not one worthy of the name the chef of the tavern had built for himself over the years.

Alwin eyed the vast food of Costace and Petra as he himself slowly nibbled at the sparse serving on his plate. Their food was inciting, fervently inviting. Envy and regret boiled in his stomach. Alwin took another swallow of his meal and tried not to hate himself for his decision. He tried not to become angry at his friends.

By the second rib, Alwin had swallowed his hateful envy. He smiled with his friends and laughed and talked as he ate slowly. Despite the size of the meal, he felt himself grow happy and full. There was no longer any pettiness in Alwin's mind. He laughed openly, a large smile planted on his face. If Alwin hadn't been enjoying himself so much, he might have noticed a pair of stern eyes boring into him, watching his every move.

Bellies full from their meals, they paid the attendant and shelled out the coin for two rooms upstairs. Costace and Petra took the larger room.

Alwin walked into his room and was greeted to a welcome surprise. Being in a corner room, Alwin faced two pairs of doors, each leading to small balconies. This was certainly better than two more walls of boarded planks. Alwin stepped out to notice his balconies were the only ones on the tavern.

Pale moonlight filled the landscape as Alwin stepped outside. He stared, peacefully, across the rolling hills of desert. Alwin took in a great breath of air and let out a soft sigh. He stood, enjoying his raised view. Life, with all its intricacies, was a delicate balance, he thought to himself.

With a calm heart and a rested mind, he took off his boots and readied himself for bed. He left the doors open to let the moonlight bathe the room in its soft glow.

A sharp knock came through his door. Alwin stood, momentarily frozen as another knock came through, calling him out.

Alwin walked towards the door, weary and curious. The wooden floor boards creaked beneath his bare feet. Alwin pulled the door back slowly and it grunted against wooden hinges.

Before him was a stooped man wearing a white, tattered jacket. The man smiled at Alwin, revealing two rows of perfectly white teeth, and motioned for him to follow. The man left, floorboards complaining as he walked away. Alwin stood clueless for a moment, then quickly decided to follow this strange man.

Alwin shadowed the man in the white coat down to the stone floor of the pub. The stone was cool against the bottoms of his bare feet. The pub was dark, save a light emanating from the kitchen and a small candle flickering atop one of the scarred, wooden tables. The man motioned for Alwin to sit. The wooden stool creaked beneath Alwin's weight as he watched the man nod and leave for the kitchen.

The man in the white coat returned with two white plates in his hands. He reverently placed them down in front of Alwin. On one plate was a single square of cornbread. On the other, a single rib, filled with meat and rubbed-on spices. Alwin stared up from the plates and looked at the chef.

"Is this for me?" He asked, hesitant.

The chef nodded, showing another warm, bright grin.

"Why?" Alwin asked.

The chef grinned again and shook his head. He opened his mouth and stuck out what was left of his tongue. Long ago, one of the jealous nobles of the Tektites cut out the chef's tongue, ensuring secrets overheard would never be told.

"Oh … well, thank you." Alwin said with a look of concern across his face. The chef patted Alwin on the shoulder and hurried behind the bar.

Alwin turned from the chef to the food in front of him. He decided first to try a square of the cornbread. He pulled a piece off and bit in. Warmth filled his mouth. The cornbread was light and airy, bursting with flavor and promise. It melted in his mouth and left him wanting more.

A clattering on the table broke Alwin out of his reverie for the cornbread.

The chef sat across from him with similar plates set in front of him and two mugs of beer. One mug was pushed over to Alwin. Alwin stared over the lip; a rich, deep, dark brew sat idling in the wooden mug. Alwin nodded in appreciation. The chef merely smiled, digging into his own plate.

The rib was covered in meat; thick, beefy, and succulent, a dry rub coated it evenly. The flesh tore away seamlessly from the bone. Alwin's tongue was soon alight with flavor from the rub, fiery but soothing and savory. Alwin relished the mouthful of meat.

The beer was full flavored, rich in aroma and texture. Alwin let out a great sigh, finishing his first gulp, and looked in astonishment at the chef sitting in front of him. He had never tasted flavors like this. His mouth watered and his mind was at a loss for words. He ate quietly and contentedly opposite the chef.

The two finished their plates and drained their beers. They stared at each other and shared a satisfied smile. They stood and shook hands. The chef began to clear their plates and Alwin offered him money. The chef shook his head, sternly refusing. Reluctantly, Alwin returned to his room, satisfied and somewhat mystified. He lay in bed, again thoughtful and full of wonder.

Refreshed from a night of deep sleep, Alwin, Petra, and Costace woke with the morning sun. They struggled into their worn road leathers, and after paying the porter for stabling their horses, set out on the next leg of their journey. To Alwin's dismay, the chef was nowhere to be seen. He had hoped to express his thanks one last time. His head full of thoughts, Alwin and his companions rode out onto the dirt road. Alwin wondered if last night's second feast had been a dream. He couldn't tell and was left with a sense of yearning, melancholy, and curiosity.

Facing the backs of the three riders was the tavern, atop the crest of a hill. It stood like it did every day, a small dot within the hopeless desert, a brief respite for weary travelers. A culinary mystery fueled by the eccentricities of its chef and owner, hidden away in one hellish strip of land covering the world.

Essays

Rachel Wyman
Pratt Institute
Winner of the 2017 Scythe Prize for Essay/Creative Non-fiction

Body Snatching/A Love Letter

muscle memory

A while ago I began envisioning backs all the time. It started with aimless doodling, then I began painting them, sculpting them in clay, and finally I set out to make a life-sized model with chicken wire and plaster. Neck (no head), shoulders (no arms), tapered torso (no pelvis). I couldn't explain why, only that each time I felt an idle creative urge, my hands went to work automatically and another back would appear. My fingers knew how gently to pinch the clay to form a spine; the shape of the back was so familiar I could feel my hand tracing it while sitting still.

You usually fall asleep before I do, and I catch myself listening to make sure your breath is regular, as I did as a kid with my parents, lying between them. Last night I also noticed myself smoothing my hands against your back, waiting for sleep to take me where you had already gone. It occurred to me that I'm always doing this – that I've been doing it for years. You might not even know, since you're elsewhere when I do my mapping.

That's what it is- not massage, but mapping. Mapping and magical thinking. I've spent years imprinting the surface of your back in my hand. Trying all the while to penetrate the outmost layer and hold you by the bones.

danger

Being a body is dangerous; I don't recommend it. I realize that if you're reading this, you are almost definitely a body. But you may also be thinking, "I *have* a body, but that's not me. *I'm* me." If that's the case, you're on the right track and I admire the way you think. I'll put it this way instead: letting that "Me" feeling settle into your body is dangerous and should probably be avoided.

By that, I mean feeling your self in your body the way your body might feel in a safe and easy place, like a childhood home. You slouch around

137

with great comfort, noticing as familiar surfaces gather dust. Familiarity, ease, tenderness – danger.

Here's a question: has a not-too-intimate acquaintance, showing her supreme trust and generosity, ever let you stay in her home for a night or two? Better to feel your body like that – very lightly, cautious, almost wary. Tread softly on the carpet. Don't open the cupboards.

I only say so because I know how easily a person attaches to those physical joys, and as everyone knows by now, attachment means suffering sooner or later. I'm attached to my body, so attached that I believe Body is all there is and all I want. I know I'd be better off as Essence or Spirit, or whatever you prefer to call formlessness that is safe from rot. The stuff that's supposed to be everlasting. Make the choice while you still can. Be Spirit. Be comforted knowing that the echo calling "I am me" from its bone cave is what makes you real, not the bones themselves.

Comfort from a stroke on the back is more complicated.

body plans

Body things can obsess a person. Both inside things like feelings, and surface things like colors, textures, the shapes of parts, and how gracefully they fit together. I've obsessed my way through the insides and outsides of my body. Just when I believe I have obsessed exhaustively, something new comes up to distress or delight me.

In fact, there is obsession now. I fantasize about being mated and impregnated, of my body making a body. I hear this is typical at a certain point in the lifespan, but I feel betrayed by my body for conjuring such a mundane plan for itself.

I tell myself I would like to live out some kind of successful adulthood. I know passing on genes isn't the only way, but I'm impressed by how hard the body fights for it. It's the most personal universal way of leaving something of yourself, because it doesn't get more personal than making a body from your body, yet almost every body on earth feels the same compulsion. I hate doing what everyone else does. I thought I had different plans for myself (I ruled out aging, dying, and procreating), but my body has hijacked those ambitions in the name of the Great Body Plan. All bodies share the same agenda.

I never knew about the agenda until I got a bit older, but I don't believe this is because the body's plan kicks in at a certain age. I think that whereas childhood is a time of more body than thought, adults experience more thought than body. A thought-full person is more likely to notice and be disturbed when her body's plan diverges from her thoughts.

I do miss that body-full time. A time of rituals instead of words.

rituals

A ritual is a body putting itself through the same motions, over and over. But what makes rituals different from routines? Some say the context and purpose: rituals are reverent and conscious; routines are dutiful and thoughtless. Rituals revolve around the invisible, like a person's soul; routines tend to the tangible, like a person's teeth.

Either way, everything happens through the body. Isn't a soul stuck in the same receptacle as the teeth? Whether it's a ritual or a routine, aren't the soul, bones, and organs all going through the motions together in one container?

I can intellectually see why candle-lighting and prayer get elevated over tooth-brushing, but it feels arbitrary.

memory muscle

There's a moment at the dinner table when it's time to get up, go to my father, and ask to be excused. The body knows when its supply of stillness has run out. Still, parents know how to prolong the supply. I stand next to him while he absent-mindedly caresses my back and continues whatever conversation is droning on. There's no such thing as waiting when you are soft, stroked, unfocused body-ness. Time suspended in the mulling over. Better than liberation.

The body is a heat-seeking missile. Invisible things like thoughts and dreams are cold. Hurry away from those intangibles where any terrible thing is possible! There is no space so safe as between bodies. Especially the bodies that made you. Warm and breathing and rhythmic in all their functions. Join the quiet symphony of heartbeats and respiration and borborygmi. I am their bodies and theirs are mine.

139

Some say they see people's energy, auras, vibrations and other useful personal information. I imagine all of this as a bunch of squiggly lines and rainbows emanating from every body, only visible to the sensitive and gifted. I'm not gifted in that way, although I'd like to be.

The body tells a lot, but evidently not as explicitly as those invisible things. Bodies speak to other bodies, in messages that have no words and appear in the head as half-formed thoughts and gobbledygook. Much of the time, I find my thoughts simply don't know.

not knowing

But then at times the body doesn't know either, as in learning sequences of movement – a dancer's choreography. The eyes see actions unfold and disappear. The body repeats what it thinks it has seen, but hasn't yet felt. The movement is moving – moving from the instructor's body, which knows and feels it, to a body that doesn't know. During that time, the movement is body-less and undefined in the space between.

The body that doesn't yet hold it moves vaguely with only the faintest hint of the movement. Repetition changes it each time. It comes slowly into the body with more volume and realization. The movement becomes clearer, boldly outlined, definite. It finally becomes a something that is consciously known to the body and mind.

The mind doesn't know when it doesn't know something. In the mind, the something stands fully in light or in darkness. Bodies move through the full spectrum of not knowing.

bones

To be honest, I'm happier without the thoughts. The human species has come so far that I'm ashamed to say I'm ungrateful for the benefits. And to have stumbled into a safe and privileged human existence at a relatively good time in history at that. I don't deny I'm an ingrate. It's just how I feel.

Maybe I would not give up the thoughts entirely. But it's so easy to lose track of reality up there, and to time-travel, and ruminate, and redo conversations and take all kinds of bold action. To inflict feelings upon the body with thoughts alone, in complete absence of external stimuli.

Happiness is body-ness. Immediate, physical, real. Eating and sexing and sweating and shitting. I'd be lying if I said I was smiling just thinking about it. I only smile while I'm doing it.

This is why I'd trade all of our words – our stimulating conversations, our pedantic arguments, our fearful confessions and murmured revelations of truth and feeling – for another few moments of soft shared body-ness. Your back breathing my belly breath. Holding you by the bones.

Christopher S. Davis
Alaska Pacific University

Dandelions

Jay's disability lies scattered somewhere between Anchorage and Nome on the Fetal Alcohol Spectrum. The alcohol took my three-year-old grandson's speech in-utero, but spared his strength and wisdom. We are casing a deserted playground; a rusty jewel ensconced in a crown of birch and fireweed. Jay loves it here. No child gates or fragile knick-knacks. No firm Grandpa voice.

I follow him to the swings then sit in one, rocking it back and forth. "This is how you swing, Jay." I try to place him onto the swing, but he resists. He places his chest onto the seat, pushes himself up with his feet and raises them, squealing with delight as he "supermans" back and forth. *This is how I do it, Grandpa.*

He soon loses interest and skitters over to a mish-mash of chutes and ladders, climbing halfway up a slide, then jumping into the pea gravel. I point to the adjacent ladder and climb to the top. "This is how you climb, Jay." I attempt to guide him to the ladder, but he wriggles free, and finds the stairs on the opposite side. He walks up to the highest step then peers down at me. *No Grandpa. This is how I do it.*

He shoots a few slides then guides us across the playground, stopping in a field of dandelions that have gone to seed. I crouch beside him, pluck a dandelion, and then blow. We both watch as the delicate seeds float away. I pluck another urging him to try and then place it into his hand. "Blow on it, Jay." He throws it to the ground and before I can become annoyed, he launches through the field into the late afternoon sun. *Billions* of tiny parachutes fly into the air behind him and he laughs while revving to greater speed. He corkscrews through the field before stopping in front of me, silhouetted by the afternoon sun and wreathed in floating dandelion 'chutes. *No Grandpa. This is how it's done.*

Mary Hess
New York University

You Must Not Eat Much, Huh?

I almost felt beautiful once.

The tight black dress finally hugged a stomach that refused to bulge and a butt that demanded to. My calves, carved out of stone, sat above four-inch heels. My skin gleamed from self-tanner and my face was caked with enough makeup to stock a Sephora.

I walked out of my room to join my family for the wedding.

"Mary, you look unbelievable," my mom said.

And I did. I finally did.

At the beginning of my second semester of freshman year, I told myself that, by the time of my cousin's wedding in May, I would be forty pounds thinner. Why? I don't know. To look good on the special day? Sure. But these games of losing and gaining weight were my favorite pastimes; stints of binging, binging and purging, binging and exercising compulsively, and starving were as constant as the seasons. I lived from one extreme to the next, changing often, like my hometown's leaves in the fall, but it was never that beautiful. So this spring, I tried something different, something fresh and new and pure, like the flowers in Washington Square Park and the promise of new beginnings. I tried being healthy.

This new adventure was exciting, compelling even. I would finally lose weight the right way and keep it off, you know, the way normal people take care of themselves. I started with my diet. Healthy people surely must have rules with what they eat. They must, otherwise they wouldn't be healthy. Rules mean you care. So I made a list of the things I could not eat, the way normal people do.

Flour? No.

Bread? Never.

White sugar? Hah.

White rice? Bye bye.

Butter? Avoid at all costs.

When I starved myself in the past, I made lists of things that I *could* eat, so this surely seemed like an acceptable balance between no rules and endless ones. I compiled a total of twenty-two things I could not, under any circumstance, eat and saved it on my computer. I could drink alcohol one night a weekend, but no flavored liquor, beer, or cocktails were allowed. Shots of tequila, gin and tonics, and red wine were acceptable. To keep my metabolism high and my body happy, I could have one meal a week that was a "cheat." Tacos, pizza, ice cream, you name it – as long it was only once.

I saved my meal plan moved on to my fitness plan. Like my meals, my workouts would be balanced so I wouldn't go overboard. I decided on six days of workouts, broken up into both cardio and lifting. Saturday was my one day of rest. I printed my guidelines out, stuck them in my notebook, and felt a strange sense of relief. I would be okay as long as I followed these rules. These rules would keep me balanced, keep me normal, and make me happy.

It started out fine. Every day I had a banana for breakfast, a salad for lunch, and veggies and fish for dinner. If I was really hungry, I could eat an apple in between meals. But I often felt full and ready for my workouts at night, which lasted for two-and-a-half hours. The routine left me euphoric, motivated, safe. I lost twenty pounds in a month.

Like things always do for me, it got extreme. I upped my gym time to four hours every night, leaving class early for "appointments" I could get to the gym at six to have enough time before they closed at ten. Friday nights, it was just me and a few older men in the cardio room, which smelled like rotting cheese and socks. I loved it. I owned that place. I ran to pop music and smirked through my sweat; other girls were out dancing to this song, but I'm getting *skinny* to it.

My salads soon became just lettuce, spinach, and any other dark green I could find. I read that broccoli and cauliflower could cause stomach bloat, so I cut those out. The hummus I'd put on my greens had too much fat in it now; the wedding was getting close and it was time to get serious.

That semester, I only went out with friends twice. I knew if I saw them, there would be alcohol. There would be bad food. I was doing myself a favor by avoiding it. Most nights, my roommate went dancing, begging me to come out with her. I'd smile, say I have too much homework, and spend the rest of the night watching Youtube videos on how to lose weight. When I got skinny, I could go out all the time like her.

I would catch myself thinking in those terms – skinny instead of healthy, thin instead of athletic. I had to remind myself that this was a health journey, yes, but of course being skinny would be a side effect to self-care. It had to be.

I worked harder and harder on my body until May 17, the day of the wedding, finally came. I bought this unbelievable, skintight black dress for the event, the kind of dress that only tiny people can pull off. And I pulled it off.

Twirling around in the mirror, my body told me I met my goal. I looked thin but healthy, athletic and glowing, beautiful. My body really did look, dare I say, *perfect*.

At the reception, my family and loved ones showered me with affection – how good I looked, if I was training for a marathon, if I could be their nutritionist. I smiled and put my hands on my hips. "Just eat healthy and exercise!" I said. "The key is balance."

When everyone lined up for the dinner buffet, I grabbed a plate and noticed an older woman staring at me. Her eyes were cloudy from too much wine.

"Wow," she said, looking me up and down. "You must really work hard for that body."

"I guess so," I replied, throwing some green beans on my plate.

"You must not eat much, huh?"

Defiantly, I heaped a mound of spaghetti on top of my green beans and just smiled back at the glassy eyed woman, as if to show off the carbs in my hands. To show her, to show everyone, that I could be beautiful and still have my cake, too.

In reality, I was fighting deep hunger pangs. I hadn't eaten all day. So, I sat down and inhaled the spaghetti. Every last bite. I couldn't remember the last time I had flour; it was wonderful. My mom sat next to me and I saw her plate was still half full. I must have eaten too fast.

"I'm hungry and I haven't eaten at all until now and it's a special event today so it's okay to have this," I said, sputtering over myself.

"Sure is," mom said, maneuvering to get a good photo of my cousin and his new wife. She didn't seem to care – rightfully so. I excused myself to the bathroom.

Looking in a different mirror, the one in this fancy restaurant, the image I saw didn't change from that morning in my room. A lot of women with eating disorders see a distorted version of themselves, but I saw the reality of it all. I saw my hard-earned body, my thin face, and the tears that fell down it. They washed away my self-tanner and foundation, leaving spots of pink flesh and mascara streaks. I felt the weight of the pasta in my stomach and the weight of everything else before I could stop it.

It was just one plate of spaghetti. But that wasn't it. That wasn't it at all.

Head in my hands, I sobbed loud and hard until a woman opened the bathroom door. I jerked up and grabbed a wad of paper towels, dabbing my bloodshot eyes, throwing on a smile.

"Wedding always make me cry," I said, laughing. I rinsed my hands and returned to the reception in my tight dress that I finally looked beautiful in.

Alexandria Redd
University of Utah

Abandoned Buildings and Crayon Drawings

An abandoned warehouse sits in the middle of a deserted property in the insignificant town of Oinofyta, Greece. The entire property is so dilapidated that the money-less Greek government doesn't even want it. Maybe the gray building was once clean, the windows clear of grime and used for its intended military purpose. But now it is forgotten, with both noticeable and hidden signs of abuse. Used, abused, and forgotten, the cycle repeating itself daily, monthly, and yearly.

As migrant camps sponsored by the United Nations are no longer able to support the continuous flow of people, there is no alternative but these discarded locations. Many overlooked sites such as this one in Oinofyta have popped up in an effort to house thousands. The Greeks toe the line between humane enough to live in, yet not quite nice enough so that the migrants ever want to stay, grudgingly fulfilling their duty as a member of the European Union.

The building I am looking at sits on a much smaller lot than most, and rightly so, since Oinofyta is an insignificant, out-of-the-way village in comparison to the many others in Thessaloniki, Athens, and Lavrio. I am not sure about the other camps, but this building is tired and it transfers its weary energy to everyone in its presence. The surrounding landscape makes the building seem even more hopeless. I am told that everything in this part of the country is either dry and sweltering or dry and freezing. Right now, the weather seems stubbornly set on dry and sweltering.

There is sandy dirt everywhere. This is not to be confused with soil-dirt. And definitely not with a sandy, beige beach. The best way to describe it is as the planet Tatooine from the Star Wars movies: a sandy dirt that is impossible to avoid, gradually coating itself onto every inch of your body. The wind blows it every which way, spitting it into your eyes every so often as a not-so-subtle reminder that this dirt is omnipresent.

Co-conspiring with the dirt is a certain stench. The smell floats from trash that is as forgotten as the building. A garbage man contracted by the government may come every so often when his heart desires it, but even then not all of the trash is taken. He gets tired in the middle of his work and says he will be back later. But the building knows he won't be back, due to the never-ending cycle of strikes. This building is deemed unworthy of cleaning up and so the smell persists.

Rotten food, old wrappers, boxes, diapers, mold, and decay are all found in this heap. Then the smell of the garbage combines with the funk of sweaty, unwashed bodies. Donations are few and far between so there is never enough soap. Most go without showering, resigned to the filth they have been covered in for months. Sometimes the sweaty bodies get sick and all three smells fuse together. There might be vomit from the foul food the Greek government delivers, or flesh being torn apart by scabies. Sores are not uncommon, and with those come another distinct aroma. The building takes the smells as yet another facet of its personality.

It is not unusual to be forgotten, as the Greek people feel the bleakness, too. Trash piles up as social upheaval, a common thing, takes workers to places like city hall instead of landfills, one recent article states. The people at the camp know there is no future for them here, as the country cannot even support its own people. Of the 50,000 migrants remaining on Greek territory, most are awaiting the outcome of asylum applications, eager to continue toward more affluent countries. But weeks and months go by with no progress made through the asylum office.

At this rate the building may never be the same.

Being surrounded and immersed in this place, with this dirt and these smells, I start to really *see*, and my conclusion is painful to admit. This gray, tattered, deserted, broken building reflects the people living inside of it. The building is tired, as are the people. The building is abused and forgotten, as are the people. The shattered windows reflect broken bones, broken families, broken hearts. The noxious odor weaving itself through the air is equivalent to the miasma of hopelessness the people breathe in and out constantly. Even the pestering dirt has meaning. It represents the unforgettable truths of their situations. This place has taken the years of neglect and maltreatment into its personality. Similarly, there is no way to shield the people from the raging windstorm of their past experiences. And so the people are, just as the building is.

The dusty clothes and faces. Some look malnourished, some sleep in any piece of shade they can find. Actions lack purpose and everyone lacks a smile. The building gives refuge and in return the refugees set about trying to beautify the lot. The residents do all they can to make this place home, to breathe life into the building and, in turn, breathe life into themselves – a symbiotic relationship. One provides protection and the other maintains; one provides warmth and the other life. They find comfort in one another through the waves of summer heat and surely the same will occur when the snows eventually fall.

The symbolism is hard to admit because to compare people to a building, especially a building such as this, is dehumanizing. Yet, what else is there?

The infuriating reality is that 23 million displaced people across the globe live as half-humans. In the past few years, the Syrian war has caught the attention of the Western media, but there are many other groups represented here. Those I have come to know here at the camp have walked about 2,500 miles from Afghanistan to Greece, only to find they have nowhere to go but this depressing, overlooked lot.

There is one area on the outside of the building that is starting to show life, however. Along the north side of the building facing the barbed-wire fence, crammed between the medical trailer and more dirt, is a section of wall no taller than four feet and no longer than seven. This section of wall is directly under the rusting window panes, but unlike the rest of the building, it has not succumbed to the red-brown drip of rust. It is not gray – worn and weathered maybe, but definitely not gray.

The reason this wall is not dead is quite simple: children and their crayons were here. There are various drawings of flowers, suns, fish. Self-portraits. Vibrant purple stick figures playing with what might be a neon green dog. Fish that are pinks and reds. Suns with what are undeniably smiley faces. Flowers that are wild shapes and sizes growing up past the stick people. Of course, some are just the scribbles of a toddler trying to keep up with the older ones.

There is not a patch that hasn't been drawn on. Even the dirt has no effect on it.

I love this wall. This wall is where I met my small friends, where we have played in the shade and sat on the cold concrete, where they have talked and I have listened. This is where my friends brought their set of brand new crayons to share with me. This is also where we got in trouble – especially me for encouraging such behavior. The adults see the graffitied wall and are incensed. "Naughty children." "Savage children." Always mad at the children and their disregard for reality. At home, I might have cared. *The audacity of drawing on walls! Vandalism!*

Here, I eagerly partake in the mischief.

We drew pictures of one another, but what struck my heart are the pictures they drew me of their stories, what has happened from Afghanistan to here, what we in the West consider "current events." Many news reports highlight these pictures: red streaks pouring from the stick people and evil looking men waving what look like knives and guns. Mountains in Iran with snow where they drew themselves without coats, shivering. Scary boat rides after arriving to the coast of Turkey with sharks circling beneath. And a colorful square they said was home. Home? This place is where they meant. This place that has been used, abused, and forgotten. This is their new home. This drawing is not dark and grim, really nothing like my description whatsoever. It shows happy stick people, playing stick people, and little stick people sliding down the mounds of dirt I once loathed. The dirt has won my heart if it can make my little friends happy.

There are many tears rolling down the faces of the adult stick figures in the pictures my sweet little ones drew of those living at the camp. The adults all look angry, sad, or straight-faced. No smiles and no sense of joy. In contrast, the pictures of the children all have smiling faces. The little stick people hold hands with their new friends, go to the tiny schoolhouse to read, and even play in the piles of sewage happily.

As adults from western countries looking at the entire refugee crisis, we wrap ourselves in the shortages and shortcomings, seeing nothing but scarcity, bloodshed, and clumsy leadership in our elected officials. Adults see the help and aid given as a drop in the bucket, meaningless, doing little to alleviate suffering. Of course, everyone must eat and have shelter and clothing. Reality is reality. Nonetheless, I think the meaning of crayons is lost on adults everywhere. Adults only choose to see what they want of the gray building, their gray building. They maintain the gray, whether they mean to or not. They have surrendered to being one with the building.

I acquiesce that crayons might not have much meaning anywhere else. But here, crayons are every sunny, hopeful cliché. These little ones live on, running every which way, playing with one another, and making noises children make. These children have not yet become abandoned buildings like the adults. Broken crayons do not reflect a broken child. Despite the realities of their situations, which I believe the children are well aware of, they have found light in a world that has been plunged in darkness. The children can be children and this wall assures their past does not become their present.

The warehouse is still broken but it has a spot of intense colors made with crayons. This piece of the building is a reflection of innocent and enduring souls. This place is proof that ugly does not mean ugly forever. This wall is hope in a world of gray buildings.

George Such
University of Louisiana Lafayette

Where's My Lunch?

I stood in the July heat outside the New Orleans airport, my backpack slung over my right shoulder. It was night already. I'd just returned from a month in Guatemala studying Spanish, but due to a delayed flight there, I'd missed my connecting flight into New Orleans from Houston. And now, several hours late, my ride to Baton Rouge was no longer available. I needed to take a cab. Public transportation is not Louisiana's forte.

A taxi pulled up and after I recovered from the shock that it was going to cost me two hundred dollars, we were on our way. The driver was from India and when he found out I'd been there several times, his manner became more relaxed. He offered me some Indian crackers from his lunch box and was genuinely excited that I'd experienced his former country – he was from Delhi. We talked at length about our times there. It was a one-hour drive.

I asked him how he liked Louisiana and he chuckled, saying he felt right at home here, as it was a lot like India.

You mean the weather?

No, I mean the way things work here – it's just like India.

How's that?

He proceeded to tell me a story about how before Katrina he had his own business in New Orleans. The climax of the story concerned the day he went with a friend downtown to get his first business license:

I gave my check for the license to the guy behind the counter, plus all the paperwork. Everything was filled out and ready to go. He looked over everything carefully and then he said to me: Where's my lunch?

I didn't know what to think. I started to give him a sandwich I had with me, but my friend put his hand on my shoulder and whispered in my ear: He doesn't want your food, he wants $100. So I slipped him a hundred dollar bill and everything went fine. Ever since then I've felt right at home here.

We both laughed.

But don't tell anyone about this, he said, turning to look back at me. I don't want to get into any trouble.

Don't worry, I told him, your secret's safe with me.

Elizabeth Ensink
Hope College

Ecosystem of Echoes

"You can only see straight ahead, but you can hear in all directions at once. Learning bird songs is a great way to identify birds hidden by dense foliage, faraway birds, birds at night, and birds that look identical to each other. In fact, when biologists count birds in the field, the great majority of species are heard rather than seen."

– The Cornell Lab of Ornithology, "Bird ID Skills"

You hear so many things in a forest instead of seeing them: the harsh pip of a chipmunk, the chirr of a red-bellied woodpecker, the impact of two dragonflies in chase like paper to a window fan. Some sounds curl through your cochlea but remain anonymous, disconnected from what you can label: the pent up chirp that bubbles out all once, the plop of something entering the creek, shifting leaves just off the trail. Disorienting, maybe, but if you choose to let them be, the sounds become a blanket, the fabric of a hike without a destination.

This blanket covers you in other spaces also, in the city streets and hallways far from the forest – the rapid click of a broken turn signal, the hum of an air conditioning unit reviving in July. The places you tread only rarely seem the loudest.

***

Nursing home sounds, for example, only become familiar over time – the clatter of the nurse's cart, high heels clicking on the tile floor when visiting after church, the crescendo and decrescendo of a conversation passing by the door, the door alarm.

When sitting with my grandma in her beige room, I wondered if the sound of that alarm ever became familiar to her. Only frequent visitors learned the password for the keypad that would silence the alarm: just the four digits of the current month and year.

But the alarm still rang almost every hour in a circular sound that looped in shrill cries each time someone entered into this place of old wounds and reunions for the first time.

I wondered if it ever actually served its purpose of keeping residents from leaving without notice; the ones who roamed the hallways in their wheelchairs, plastic grey handrails as their safety line. I don't know how many actually tried to sneak out; I know my grandma never left her room. When I try to picture her now, I can only think of the photographs at her funeral and the blankets around her body, but the soundscape of the nursing home still reverberates in my mind- a tympanic membrane of memory, tapping.

***

It is easy to forget that the trees are alive, but when the wind bends and flows through their branches, it reminds me that they are always moving. The young, thin-trunked trees are the most aggressive. Their crowns knock together in a series of impacts: the tips of trunks, then branches, then twigs – a concave tap then splinters of sound like drumming fingers. With such force, I expect a sort of tumbling, but only a single leaf floats down, settling on the ground long after the trees have stilled. Often, the waves of leaf-flutters wash over this wooden sound unless you listen for it. In this way, the wind becomes white noise of the woods, though I don't know whether this sound belongs to the trees or the wind since each relies on the other to be heard.

The oldest trees are more careful in their creaks like the smooth curve of rocking chair feet leaning back to ruminate on rings of wisdom. I suppose the creak of a rocking chair is an exact echo of the trees' sound in a reincarnation of the wood supporting a lifetime of growth.

But the pair of chairs in my grandparents' trailer home were the gliding, cushioned sort with wood hidden under golden tan fabric and batting. And I'm not sure when the swaying of wood was equated with wisdom. The floor did creak though, in the shuffle of arrival after the three hour drive to Michigan. We always hugged Grandpa first, in his baseball cap with the mesh netted back, sometimes fiddling in the shed outside and other times watching the news. Grandma was usually at the stove, stirring a pot or carefully spreading a pat of butter across a loaf of bread, stretching the melted yellow across as much surface area as possible before it disappeared. But often they were at the door before we were so that any glimpse of their life apart from our visits was lost in greetings.

***

How many others have written about the woodpecker's knock, the wind in the leaves, and the whippoorwill? Maybe this is only an echo without the true timbre. My grandparents, too, are at risk of being reduced to a monophonic recording, a single track of hugs and grey hair that could belong to anyone. It is so easy to level out all the spikes and dips into a single warm tone, but symphonies require discord and resolution.

I struggle to remember what my grandma wore while standing at the stove when we would visit, but I do remember the robotic ribbit of the plastic frog triggered by our footsteps as we arrived and left. My brother and I would try to hop over it, gleeful when we tricked it, confused when it would croak moments later with no one in its path. And there was the phone magnet among all the others on their pale yellow fridge – wooden shoes, shopping cart, windmill. The phone magnet was no bigger than the palms of our grade-school hands but you could press the receiver and make it ring, a high-pitched but blurry trill, and we'd giggle when my grandma would start out of her seat to answer it.

"Oh for cat's sake," she'd say.

And there was the train lumbering by on the tracks just outside their window.

We'd hear the rumble first and run to the window to count the cars, comparing answers when the last one rolled by. And above the ceramic goat named Oscar, there was the deep green clock with woodland birds instead of numbers, though I only remember hearing it chirp out the hours once.

But these sounds are real too: my grandmother, the last night I saw her, not whispering I love you, last advice, or psalms, but pleas to relieve the phantom pain in her legs: "leg up, leg up." My dad and uncle stood at the foot of her bed, each lifting one of the lumps rocking under the blanket.

"Mom, is that better?" Moans. Gagging on her plastic teeth and pain medication. Gargling on the water she couldn't swallow. The murmur of nurses offering snacks to her neighbors next door who could still eat.

***

Suppose I was to envision instead the gargle of a gentle creek where the water runs up against a sodden log and finds a way under or over. What if I were to transform the alarm into a field sparrow's gentle bouncing trill outside her window or imagine a quiet reminiscing of her kindness instead of the misplaced conversations in the hallway about college plans or nurses explaining catheter options.

I was not at the nursing home to hear it, but my mom told me that just the day before, Grandma talked with her aunt for over an hour. My mom said she couldn't follow their conversation, their reminiscing on a past she knew nothing about. But they laughed. I can't remember my grandma laughing now and I don't know if this is a failure of memory or absence of the event. Suppose I let these sounds be a part of my memory also, though I can't quite identify where they come from. Would this be a fraud? Many artists create mix-tapes or covers of songs more beautiful than the original. Maybe they are just like the sounds in the forest that I can locate but not identify; the kind I want to listen to on repeat to understand.

***

How quickly the soundscape changes. A few steps out of the trees, scrubby wood opens onto grasses and ferns next to wetlands. The syncopated rustle of squirrel leaps in leaf litter are replaced by the muffled slide of a snake below matted down fibers. Everything is more still out in the open. When it begins to rain, the frogs strike up conversation like banjo strings. You can only feel these raindrops, see the pricks on the lake as if you are water. You miss the sound of it pattering a glass surface, but this rain is the silent kind. The great majority of things are felt rather than heard.

Krystal Lau
University of California- Los Angeles

With The Same Lungs

Walk into my house and you might feel like you're teleporting to another country. The TV's playing the Chinese news network, the table's set with chopsticks, and tai chi music issues from the backyard. You won't be wearing shoes because you'll have taken those off by the door.

This was my "American" childhood.

Growing up, I ate fried chicken with chopsticks. I learned zodiac animals before I even knew what the word "horoscope" meant. I was never acquainted with Miley Cyrus or her country-rock alter-ego until coming to college in LA. I didn't receive allowance, but I did look forward to Lunar New Year when my relatives gave me lucky red envelopes full of dollar bills.

Needless to say, I never really struggled with feeling whitewashed or assimilated into mainstream American culture. Instead, I couldn't help but feel Chinese. On the surface, I was – milky skin, pitch hair, almond-shaped eyes. And yet, something within me was shifting, changing to fit the mold of my American peers. As I left home to attend preschool, then elementary school, then high school, I started to take on the beliefs and ideas of my contemporaries and teachers. There I learned that independence was key, that individualism allows for success, and that to get to the top, you have to fight for it on your own. These explicit school teachings clashed with the tacit, unspoken teachings of my family and culture – that the well-being of the community is more important than the individual and that quiet persistence rather than loud attention-seeking will take you further.

It was like trying to sew together two pieces of unmatched fabric; inevitably the thread got tangled. Something intuitive and inborn within me shrunk from this American ideal of individualism; it felt viscerally wrong to me in a way I couldn't explain. When I accompanied my dad on his doctor rounds to the nursing homes, I would see dozens of grandparents, alone and unwanted, wasting away on sawdust chicken and afternoon sitcoms. Now in college, when tuition payments come around, I hear of friends struggling with student loans, while their parents are more than capable of chipping in to cover the costs. This fend-for-yourself mentality seemed mercenary, unsustainable. It isn't something I want for myself, for my own family.

158

And yet, all the same, I resented the constant pressure tugging me towards the collectivist culture within my community – the need to share every detail of my life, to chart my life course around my family's well-being, to never be separate but always whole. I wanted one thing and then I wanted another. I was content. Then I was restless.

Living in China only exacerbated my sense of unbelonging. For many summers, when I would stay in Shanghai, I would hear my Chinese friends and relatives say things that made me deeply uncomfortable, holding standards that I did not adhere to. These individuals would approve of my height and my long legs, and then, in the same breath object to my using them; when they heard that I ran a half-marathon, they would try to dissuade me from using my body in a manner unfit for women.

When I would go shopping in the outdoor markets, I could never speak – my accent would give me away and mark me as a foreigner, which would inevitably increase the price. Some of my Chinese friends even tried to imitate my accent, thinking that the American accent was "cute" and "girly." Despite their compliments and good intentions, their way of thinking still set me apart, making me into the foreigner, the "other."

The worst, though, was the unashamed and blatant sexism. One time, I saw a newsreel describing a Chinese boss's habit of having all female workers line up to kiss him every morning at the start of the workday. The Chinese man claimed to have picked up this practice from the States.

The soap operas and miniseries all broadcast on the main television channel and depicted scenes of feminine weakness, men in shining armor needing to come rescue them. And beyond the screen in reality, if a woman passed the age of thirty still unmarried, she was labeled a *sen nu*, a "leftover woman" – undesirable and looked down upon. Never mind that more Shanghai women were choosing to forego marriage in order to have a career – the stigma remained. In fact, that very choice of career over marriage demonstrated that the two were not compatible, that a Chinese woman could not have one without the other. If she chose a husband, the man expected her to relegate all other activities as secondary to the family.

So it's safe to say I did not fully conform to the norms and beliefs of mainland China either. Existing in a kind of halfway between, I floated in liminal space, trapped between cultures. After getting caught in the waves– pushed and pulled by the tide– I washed up on an island of my own making.

I think, in a way, this is what it means to be Asian American. To be neither here nor there, but to fit in. And not with a geographical boundary, but with group of people sharing the unique experience of attempting assimilation into a country that can never become your own.

The truth is, you can read every Hollywood gossip rag and watch every primetime sitcom. You can take on a diet of purely french fries and apple pie, and you can even dye your hair to straw and cake your skin with white powder– ultimately, you're still different. There's always going to be something that sets you apart. You can't change where you came from. You can't change where your family came from. And try as you might, you can't change your blood.

Coming to terms with this sometimes feels like walking a tightrope, balancing on the fraying wire and knowing one misstep can force you off the line. Living this double identity means being extra careful, extra aware. It means navigating the space between forgetting how to speak the language of your ancestors and overusing that same language to the point that non-speakers feel excluded. It means not being ashamed of hanging out with friends of your own background, but also building relationships and listening to perspectives outside of that culture even though it might be more comfortable to just stay with those who understand. And that's the thing – that's why it's so hard; it's nearly impossible for someone outside of this collective experience to understand. How can you explain what it feels like to hear praise after praise for your pale skin, when all you've really wanted for years has been to be tan like your best friend? How can you explain what it feels like to be scolded for being loud by your relatives, and then in the same day be labeled quiet by your friends? How can you simultaneously live, and even thrive, under the judgments and standards of two distinct cultures? How can you breathe in open air and underwater with the same lungs?

I have no answer; I'm still trying. But things are looking up. The other day, I was having dinner at a restaurant when I overheard the table next to me struggling to communicate with their waiter. I intervened, and translated a few phrases for them. After the waiter left, one of the Chinese girls turned to me and said, "Wow, your Chinese is so good!"

A little while later, the waiter returned to take my order. After collecting the menus, he turned to me and said, "Wow, your English is so good!"

I can't deny the unmistakable tone of surprise in both of their voices, but I can say it is nice to be appreciated sometimes. Whatever the reason.

160

Jake Dardzinski
Western Washington University

A Writer's Path

You'll begin with an idea. Sometimes it comes in a dream, spellbinding. Other times a stranger, a single sentence overheard, not meant for your ears but finding its way to you nonetheless. Sometimes, it will be a singularity. Others, a kaleidoscope of ideas fused into one wondrous collage.

Regardless of how the idea got there, it will grow within you. It can be a slow process, but the result is inevitable; it overcomes you, consumes you, ravages you until put into words. Like the first gasp for air after a long time submerged, it fills you with life. A new purpose drives your fingers to move at unholy speeds and you work with a single-minded determination.

For the first chapter, nothing else matters. You know nothing but the story; enraptured by the world you have birthed. Oftentimes, so beset you'll be with inspiration you'll complete the first chapter in one swift motion. All that matters is that moment of completion, the beginning of something new. You have entered a deep forest and all you have to guide you is your dream, or the voice of a stranger uttering a revelation, or the whisperings of a million little ideas. It will be frightening to you, the possibilities behind each passing leaf, but you will forge ahead because you know you must.

Now, your inspiration will become a moon that waxes and wanes. You may go weeks without touching pen to paper, but sometimes you will find yourself bathed in midnight's light, writhing with new ideas. Possessed by the spirit of inspiration, you will write with fervor until the sun kisses your weary eyes and reminds you to rest. For you the best part of writing a novel is the first draft, and that is understandable; it is all you know. For now, the thrill of meandering down a path which builds itself before your eyes is singular. You do not look behind to see the paths untaken, shrouded by the undergrowth; ones that will certainly lead to vast, heart-stopping vistas and the introduction of new faces. The discovery of these paths will come later for you, when you wander backwards through your trails, searching the bushes for rotten berries and planting the seeds for new life.

As you write, you'll invariably come face to face with a boogeyman you've heard much about. It will appear to you as a wall of broken, brick bodies and stony semblances, and you'll be petrified by fear. You'll see, in those craggy faces, the stories of those that came down this path before and were stopped dead by the fear of progress. They plant their feet and promise to continue onwards as soon as they receive a revelation that will never come. The worlds they built crumble into disarray and all that remains is their fractured visage serving as a reminder to those who too wander these paths. You are mightier than this wall of the lost and you break through to the other side, path spilling out into the forest of ideas.

You'll learn that all things come to an end. With your heart aflutter you will pour your soul into the final few words, diligently ensuring they stay with the reader for the remainder of their days. With a sigh, you will realize what you have accomplished and you will step out of the forest, turn back, and see how inviting it has become. With a smile, you will enter the forest once more, free to run with reckless abandon down a path you once believed to be fraught with perils of the unknown. This is the first time you'll be able to look upon the path you created and float down free as the breeze.

This is only the beginning of your journey though it feels like the end. Like the first time you began your path, you will not know the way. But even in the darkest depths of the woods, the sunlight is only just behind the leaves. With the sun comes direction and with direction comes purpose. With purpose, you forge ahead.

Hayley Bowen
Black Hills State University

Just Like Last Time

This will be the last time. You swear it.

But isn't every time the last time?

Your knees are sore from kneeling on the stony bathroom tiles and your face is cold against the edge of the porcelain bowl. Your throat is searing hot, scratchy from the acid that ravages the raw flesh of your esophagus every day. You taste the coppery tang of blood and for a moment you feel afraid that perhaps this time you have finally ripped your throat clean open like they always told you would happen, but you glance down and see that you've just added a new cut where your pale knuckles connect with your teeth. You didn't go too far.

This time.

And this is the last time.

The tape that holds your feeding tube in place against your cheek (running up your nose and all the way through your stomach so that you can't evacuate the sludge it pumps into your body) pulls at the fine grey down-like layer of lanugo on your skin- your body's last ditch attempt at trapping in heat.

You heave yourself up off the floor, leaning on the basin of the sink for support. You're shaking, all your muscles weak, exhausted, and starving. You don't have the courage to look at yourself in the mirror. You don't want to know how bad it's gotten. You don't really care because it's not bad enough.

You drag legs that used to allow you to dance across a stage down white carpeted hallway. You always hated your legs anyways. Your mouth tastes foul and you suppress a disgusted shudder at the strange dissociated knowledge of what you've become.

But that was the last time anyways.

Your mom is sitting at the kitchen table. Her face is rigid, her cheeks are flushed. You see her eyes dart back and forth across your whole body, at least what is left of it at this point. Across from her a place is set; a slab of

163

prime rib, mashed potatoes with a lake of butter atop the white mounds, and sautéed asparagus. It used to be your favorite meal, one you only had on special occasions. Your head spins at the sight and smell but you feel nauseated.

Your mother sternly orders you to sit and, apathetically, you obey. She hurls more empty threats at you- *in-patient* this, *pulled out of school* that, no more friends, no more boyfriend. Whatever. She continues to talk-yell-beg at you but you're distracted by the clip you have behind your ear that stops the toxic mush from flowing through the tube; it aches where it is pressed against your skull, pinned and hidden behind your thin fraying hair.

You realize you zoned out of your mother's lecture when you catch her looking at you expectantly. You don't have the energy to ask her to repeat herself. She stands up, thrown into a fit of rage and sadness and frustration that you can only imagine sympathizing with, and she wraps her fists around your upper arms (and you feel satisfied when her fingers overlap her thumbs) and pulls you to your feet. Despite you having at least 14 inches of height on her, she lifts you with ease and pulls you back down the grey hallway into the darkness of the stark cold bathroom.

Your head always feels foggy when you stand up these days but clarity slaps you hard in the face when you're suddenly staring at the image of some sort of devilish ghoul.

Sunken and sallow cheeks, grey eyes where you're sure green ones used to reside, and cracked pale lips that used to be soft and pink. The hair that used to be so thick it fought being held up in high tight buns now hangs limp and lifeless, draped across collar bones so sharp you wonder if they would break through the skin. You realize your mother has left your side, but she shortly returns with a photo album.

All the photos depicted a girl floating on the tips of her toes across a lighted stage, full white tutu delicately resting atop lean but visibly strong legs. Even in motion and beneath the silk of her tights and leotard you recognize the athleticism and for a confusing moment you feel jealous of her. You recognize her face and remember how much you hated those legs. Suddenly, hot tears roll down your cold face. You are so sad for her. She was so happy, so full of life; her eyes were as bright as the future of endless possibilities that existed for her. You miss her dearly.

You return your gaze to the stranger – the monster – behind the glass. It is crying too. Eyes ablaze with tears standing out sharply against the deathly pallor of the skin stretched too tight around its skull. For the first time in as long as you can remember your suffocating apathy is replaced by something else- despair and longing and anger and regret.

Your mother is crying silently. She is too tired to plead with the monster any longer.

You are exhausted. You, just this moment, become aware of how tired you are. Tired of the daily frantic battle you have with the monster that wants you to die and the girl on the stage who wants so badly to be alive again. You are so tired of this pathetic limbo of existence, and a limbo is all it will ever be. Avoiding every single thing that makes the world worth being in can scarcely be called a life.

Your heart aches in your chest, yearning so desperately to scream at the girl in the photos to never follow the monster down this path. You know she is years away and, by the time she hears you, it will be too late.

Still crying, you once again join your mother at the kitchen table. The potatoes slide all too easily down your throat. The meat melts in your mouth, sickeningly savory. Your stomach stretches and aches, unused for so long, it barely remembers how to function.

For the first time in two years you clear your plate. And for the first time in three years you're proud of yourself for it. For the first time in eighteen months your mom looks happy when she smiles and tells you she loves you.

Your hunger for emptiness and darkness has been replaced with an unquenchable thirst for life. Your eyes seem a little brighter. A little greener. Could that be…hope?

You stand and feel a less foggy than you did before. You head back to your bedroom. Down the stairs, last door on the left.

But you turn one door too early, into the bathroom.

This will be the last time.

You swear it.

Carter Vance
Carleton University (Canada)

Fainting Distance

It always starts somewhere: that glance across party rooms, an awkward handshake, your mutual friend's introduction or, increasingly, some popup on a screen. Those smooth bits of digital code hold out a kind of promise when you're in a new and unfamiliar place. It says you've been noticed. It says you're alright enough that someone is willing to take that jump, spending an evening with you, hoping for something great.

London: an internship and foundation grant, ten weeks sharing a Docklands Light Rail car with half the world's population, cramped in a youth hostel of mostly New Labour professional types. I'd switched the location on my long-unchecked OkCupid profile for the occasion, telling myself I didn't think much of it, but holding out a weird kind of hope that everything might work out this time. London had everyone from every land of the dead empire in its sprawl and, surely, one of them might take that jump with me.

I suppose that now is as good a time to mention that being asexual, my exact form of "jump" isn't the same as others. Much of my hesitance in meeting people the traditional way, and otherwise subsequent general lack of success in this realm, has come a kind of fear of misperception. Short of wearing a sandwich board reading "no sex, please," the mystification of human interaction makes broaching the subject in bald terms quite a challenge. Online dating, flawed as it might be, at least allows for an accepted degree of upfront discretion about these aspects of preference that most of us would be too polite to bring up at the outset of a potential relationship. Even in a city of 12 million, the chance of randomly meeting another of the roughly 1 percent of the population that is asexual is quite remote, so, we entrust our fates to the mystery of match algorithms and paradoxical honesty that keyboards and screen names allow.

Between work, museums, and concerts, not to mention the unfortunate incident of losing my wallet in a foreign country, I'd managed to schedule a couple of dates for the first five weeks. Both had fallen through in that odd way that makes you believe you did something terribly wrong without knowing exactly what it was. Though I would idly click about whilst waiting for the train and tube, I'd basically given up the serious possibility of finding someone. I was half-resigned to mere fun evenings for the

166

rest of my time in the Great Wen. It was then that one of those hopeful popups came to me.

Being a chronic self-doubter, I suppose I'll always wonder what it was that stuck out for her, but, never one to argue with luck's blessings, I was greatly enthused to meet. It wasn't the most auspicious of first encounters, involving a number of digital iterations of that London proverb "due to a train fault," a rather bad decision to run full-tilt to meet-up on a midsummer's noon culminating in a fainting spell (on my part) in the middle of the standing section of Shakespeare's Globe. What I most remember though, is her waiting with me in the heat stroke recovery room and the look of utterly genuine concern and empathy she wore. It was then I knew there was something to her. To London. To all of it. Something felt deeper, more real than what had come before in my life.

From there, I don't think I'd ever seen or wanted to see so much of someone over such a short period of time. It is in that whirlwind of days out in parks, of nights of meetings for tea, that it was possible to believe in the tales of what big cities do to young hearts.

And yet, just as quick, it was over; there were conferences in York, PHD theses at King's College, degrees and bills and lives to go back to for the autumn. On the last time we were together, I felt only one thing had lacked resolution: I thought about kissing her, then thought better of it.

Maybe in a former age I would have, not knowing if I'd ever have the chance again, but it is that same force of technological hope that assures us there can always be a next time. We can always message instantly and expect a reply within days at most. We can see the evolution of haircuts, event attendance, new victories and defeats at the press of a touch screen. In one sense, what might have been called a fling or summer love now never has to end, the other person can always there with us, just a "hey, how are you?" away.

In another sense, though, all things end and there is little sense in trying to deny this. Indeed, it is in the afterlife of sudden things that thought starts to actually focus on meaning. Being swept up in the dodgy shade of Haringey evenings, of the utter impossibility of meeting someone you feel strongly connected to in perhaps the world's most anonymizing city, plays a funny trick of forever on the mind.

It's easy to believe that "progress" holds our salvation, whether from climate change, car accidents, or lonesome nights, but this ignores the fact that technology is crafted by human hands and, moreover, is used by them. New platforms promise interaction that is more meaningful because it is more advanced, but *what* we share through them is ultimately the same as it ever was. We have pictures and timelines and video and audio, but in the end, the loss caused by distance still stings. Clutching parchment to one's chest in the night is scarcely different than doing so with an iPhone.

It is often said that my generation has much of our love lives modulated by the ever-present hum of technology. The outside observer might conclude that these loves are not so much of another person, but of glass and microchips. We are falling in love, lust, or some ever-intermingled combination of the two not with the person before us, but with what we perceive them to be in the self-editing funhouse mirror of the digital world. The sort of writing stemming from this hypothesis has a tone of nothing so much as the street corner apocalyptic, foretelling the end of human intimacy writ-large and the emergence of purely transactional relationship forms. Though this narrative is convenient, the facts on the ground speak to something quite different.

More than anything, technology is a perilous and imperfect scaffold we use in an attempt to transcend those borders which have always made a mockery of deeper plans. As long as human beings have travelled between places without the intent of staying, we have found these affections that have been characterized by a kind of mutually-known impermanence. The best, or rather less neurotic, amongst us are able to embrace that impermanence as part of the thrill; at least that is what they say.

I often find myself thinking that if all lost lovers between the invention of the human heart and sufficiently widespread DSL access had the option of adding each other on Facebook, most of them would. The feeling of being forever apart, or at least dependent upon the courage of the local postal carrier to fan a flicker of connection, can drive one mad, or into the arms of the convenient nearby comfort. It could be said that knowing these things to have a potential of being but once might have intensified the feelings involved. Now we draw back slightly, not wanting to seem uncouth or uncool. This same hesitance, though, impairs our connections. We draw out feelings. A burst of activity rationed over those exchanges of canned reactions and phrases of our favoured digital spaces.

I don't know where that leaves us in the wider sense. Perhaps we are doomed to exist in this between space of lost and found as long as travel and technology hold out the hope of more permanent connection. Perhaps we can reconceive of love as something which requires less of a physical sense of "being there." Perhaps, we can live again with the spirit of life and of interesting adventures, not standing too close to the glancing encounters. I particularly doubt the last of those, though.

As for myself, when I finally gathered the wherewithal to continue from that summer: I wrote a letter with an invitation to vacation together, I boxed it up with some particularly tacky emblems of Canadian pride and I sent it by post; the brown paper covering crackled with immediacy.

Editor profile

Eric Forrest is the creator, publisher, and editor of the Scythe Prize series. Through his publishing company, he's released the 2016 and 2017 editions of the Scythe Prize and a children's book he created for his daughter.

He received degrees from the University of Nebraska-Omaha in journalism and secondary English education, and has been the editorial manager of several websites, an advocate for displaced animals, the underprivileged, premature babies, The Omaha Public Library system, and education. He teaches very important short story classes to people very important to him.

Forrest is a husband, son, brother, godfather, uncle, great uncle, and father. He lives in Omaha, Nebraska with his wife, Rachel, and his children, Kate and Andrew. He is most comfortable within stacks of books.

Judge profiles

Steve Langan received degrees from the University of Nebraska Omaha and the University of Iowa Writers' Workshop, where he received the Paul Engle Postgraduate Fellowship from the James Michener Foundation. He is the author of *Freezing, Notes on Exile and Other Poems, Meet Me at the Happy Bar*, and *What It Looks Like, How It Flies*. Langan's poems appear in a variety of journals, including the *Kenyon, Gettysburg, Chicago, Colorado, North American, Notre Dame* and *Southern Humanities Reviews*...and *Fence, Verse, Jacket, Slope, Pool* and *Diagram*. He teaches at the University of Nebraska Omaha MFA in Writing program, and he is founder and director of the Seven Doctors Project, a Nebraska Writers Collective program.

www.poetryfoundation.org/poems-and-poets/poets/detail/steve-langan

Laura Marlane is the Executive Director of the Omaha Public Library, a twelve branch system serving the citizens of Omaha and Douglas County. Laura has 31 years of experience working in academic, research, and public libraries, in a variety of capacities ranging from systems administrator to director. She received her B.A. in English from Rhode Island College, and her MLIS from the University of Rhode Island. Sharing the joy of reading with others has been a life-long passion.

Matt Mason has won a Pushcart Prize and two Nebraska Book Awards; was a Finalist for the position of Nebraska State Poet; and organized and run poetry programming with the U.S. Department of State in Nepal, Romania, Botswana, and Belarus. He has over 200 publications in magazines and anthologies, including Ted Kooser's *American Life in Poetry* and on Garrison Keillor's *Writer' Almanac*. His most recent book, *The Baby That Ate Cincinnati*, was released in 2013. Matt lives in Omaha with his wife, the poet Sarah McKinstry-Brown, and daughters Sophia and Lucia.

http://matt.midverse.com

Thank you to the supporters of the 2017 Scythe Prize who care about the creation of art and its value:

Abel Djendoh

Faye Beales

Chad Broughman

Jonathan Ormsbee

Alan Harris

Lynn Bolay

Susan Pinquoch

Steve Lorenz

Shelley Wilson

Kathy Anderson

Jen Brown

Carol Dennison

Nancy Hornig

Sunny and Kevin Forrest

Linda Trout

Stacey Arehart

Sue Paintin

Gloria Kaslow

Marilyn Slavin Konigsberg

Kris O'Neil

Kathie Golden

Yozue Davila

Frederick Tran

Ryan and Kristi Forrest

Chuck and Sherry Forrest

Heather and Jeff Patora

Harriet Major

Deb Barelos

CPSIA information can be obtained
at www.ICGtesting.com
Printed in the USA
LVOW12s1140070917
547717LV00001B/3/P